THUNDERSHINE

THUNDER

SHINE

TALES OF METAKIDS

DAVID SKINNER

ILLUSTRATED BY KEVIN SKINNER

SIMON & SCHUSTER BOOKS FOR YOUNG READERS

SIMON & SCHUSTER BOOKS FOR YOUNG READERS
An imprint of Simon & Schuster Children's Publishing Division
1230 Avenue of the Americas, New York, New York 10020

SIMON & SCHUSTER BOOKS FOR YOUNG READERS is a trademark of Simon & Schuster.

Book design by Lily Malcom
The text for this book is set in Utopia.
The illustrations are rendered in charcoal.
Printed and bound in the United States of America

10 9 8 7 6 5 4 3 2 1
Library of Congress Cataloging-in-Publication Data
Skinner, David, 1963-
Thundershine : tales of metakids / David Skinner.—1st ed.
            p.   cm.
Contents: As true as she wants it—Walk this way—Poof Poof Ya does me a favor—
Meta human.
Summary: A collection of four stories about young people with extraordinary
powers, including a girl who talks with the planet Pluto, a girl who can alter reality
by redrawing maps, and a girl who can change shape.
ISBN 0-689-80556-X
1. Extrasensory perception—Juvenile fiction. 2. Science fiction, American.
3. Children's stories, American. [1. Extrasensory perception—Fiction.
2. Science fiction. 3. Short stories.] I. Title. II. Skinner, Kevin, ill.
PZ7.S6278Th 1999
[Fic]—dc21
98-29250

FOR WHEN THEY ARE OLDER

I thank my brother Kevin for the great illustrations, and my editor, David, for welcoming this union of Kevin's work and mine.

CONTENTS

WHAT IS A METAKID?

A METAHUMAN IN JUNIOR HIGH.

AND WHAT IS A METAHUMAN?

A HUMAN WITH POWERS, YOU SEE.

SOMEONE WHO IS HUMAN—

AND MORE BESIDES.

"IN FRONT OF ME EVERYTHING WAS NORMAL—EXCEPT, OF COURSE, FOR THE FLOATING COUNTRIES AND THE DOUBLE SHADOWS."

As True As She Wants It

She calls herself Jenny With a J. As if she could be Jenny With a Q or Jenny With a T. I don't know how you could spell Jenny *without* a J, but that's what Jenny calls herself. With a J. Jenny Withajay.

So Jenny Withajay is my best friend. Sort of. I have other friends and she has other friends, but none of her friends are friends with my friends and, so, Jenny and I are like the only connection between half the school and the other half. There must be something best about that. We're a pair, and pairs never get by on being only so-so. Not as I see it, anyhow.

And as I see it, best friends don't do what Jenny did.

I don't mean the thing with the maps. It was because of the maps, sure, but what she did with the maps she did to the whole world. What she did to *me* was something else altogether.

◆ ◆ ◆

Jenny Withajay's been drawing maps since forever. She knew how to spell *cartographer* even before first grade, and because she could go on and on about longitudes and latitudes and Mercator, they thought she was some sort of genius. Turns out she just knew maps. She couldn't spell *apple* on a dare, she couldn't add numbers if they weren't in degrees, and the only things she could draw were straight lines and coastlines.

She's been limping through school ever since.

At least she's learned how to spell, more or less, and add okay, and if nothing else she's gotten really good at drawing fjords and archipelagos.

A long time ago, though, she kind of ran out of things to map. You can map the world only so many times. France is always next to Spain, and Mexico is always under Texas—at least until there's a war or some such thing. Jenny was thrilled when the Soviet Empire fell. She was redrawing Eastern Europe for weeks. But then everything settled down and, well, Jenny got bored. Even mapping the Moon and the planets didn't help.

She didn't draw another map for five years.

Then she dug out the maps she had made when she was little, maps of her room and her house and her yard and our street and my yard and my house and my room. These were some of the first maps she had ever made. They weren't her best, though, and so she decided to fix them, make them neat and accurate, make them truer all around.

I wish she had left them alone.

♦ ♦ ♦

You know, one of the strangest things was that I was the only one who realized anything was wrong. I mean, Jenny knew, too, of course, since she was the cause of it all, but no one else had any idea. It could just be because we're friends and whatever happens or not to Jenny happens or not to me. Pairs get the same treatment from the world, I guess.

Anyhow, one day she came into my house, just to hang out, and when she asked if she could make new maps of everything, I said no problem. I *was* surprised that she was mapping again. I asked her why and she said why not? Fair enough.

I followed her around my house while she sketched the locations of rooms, closets, stairs, and halls. We chatted while she sketched—nothing big, this, that—Did you see what Katrina did? and Can you believe what Ryan did! I told her it was getting boring, walking around my own house, but she said it was important and I figured it was okay after all, since we talked just as well as we would have sitting on my bedroom floor.

A couple of days later, on the bus, she was really agitated, like she'd just missed getting killed or something. She asked me if I knew who she was. It was creepy, because she really meant it. She was so afraid I might not know who she was. I told her she was Jenny. She said, "With a J, right?" Yeah, I said. Jenny Withajay. Who else?

"Okay, okay," she said. "My mom and dad said the same thing." She bit her lip and then whispered, "You know how when you come into my house, through the front door?"

"Yeah."

"Which side is the kitchen?"

"Huh?"

"Which way do you go to get to the kitchen?"

"The left. In the back."

"Behind the living room."

"Yeah."

"I thought so."

You know, we are all a little weird, but you could say Jenny has more than her share of weirdness. I like her that way, but then I'm her friend. And I know that most of the time she's just performing. Sometimes, though, it *is* hard to tell. She might really believe she has a soul made of mints. She might really believe that throwing rocks allows them to sing. She tells me the dirty clothes in her room refuse to be moved and since she can't ignore the will of dirty clothes, the dirty clothes stay on her floor. Last week she wrote an entire English essay in this code that she made up as she went along, and she attached a key to the essay, with clues like, "*KG* means either *dog* or *fish*, depending on the words around it," and she was surprised when she got in trouble for it. At least she *seemed* surprised.

But I didn't think she was pretending now, with all these questions about her name and her house. Of course, Jenny being Jenny, she didn't explain herself, not even when I pressed her.

Fine, I said. Be that way.

I let her stew all day in her unexplained crisis. If she wasn't going to tell me, well, that's Jenny, and fine, that's okay. I was used to it and to be honest I didn't mind. We often spend hours ignoring each other. There's always the next day to be friends.

So first she had dismapped her own house. She told me that she didn't mean to. She just had an urge to make the map a little *different*. She had never really made make-believe maps before. I'm not sure why. You might think she's just the type to whip up imaginary countries and kingdoms. I once asked her why she never had and she just said, "At least my maps are true," as if nothing else was.

But whatever made her dig up these old maps, also made her *distort* them. As I said, it was an urge. She dismapped her own house, putting stairs in places they weren't, and rooms in places they weren't, and closets and halls in places they weren't, and when she was done she decided she wanted something to eat and so she left her room and headed for the kitchen—but no part of the house was where it used to be. Wherever things weren't, they now *were*.

Jenny had changed her house by changing her map.

And no one in her family even noticed.

The next day, in our talk on the bus, I confirmed for Jenny that her kitchen was supposed to be on the left, in the back, behind the living room. Unlike her family, I remembered the truth. And so, because I remembered, Jenny decided to experiment on me. Me, her best friend. Oh, yeah, you bet she had just gotten terrified to *death* by what she had done to her *own* house, yet she still goes and decides to dismap *mine*. Sometimes the girl just doesn't *think*, you know?

So after school, while she's at her house and I'm at mine, I'm just walking to the family room to watch TV and I pass the basement door and the basement door *disappears*. My brain screamed at me that something wasn't right but it didn't know what to make of it at first, since my brain, like most people's, isn't used to disappearing doors. I stopped and looked and saw that the door had actually moved to a different wall. For a second I was relieved, as if it's okay for doors to *move*, as long as they don't out and out *disappear*. Then, of course, my brain started screaming again.

And as I stood there I saw the family room shuffle to the right and the kitchen reshape itself and some of the windows jump to other walls. My mom was stirring a pot at the stove and she didn't notice a thing. My brother was eating chips in front of the TV and he didn't notice a thing.

Then there's a frantic banging at the back door and I thought, Oh, *man*, this is *it*, my house mutates and then the monsters come. Monsters don't usually knock, though, not even loudly. When I didn't answer the door my mom says, "Laurie, don't just stand there," but I still didn't answer it and so she says, "Hey, Earth to Laurie," but by then the monster had gotten impatient and come in on its own. It was Jenny.

She looked around and she was *not* terrified. In fact, when she realized that my house was changed, she was downright gleeful. She waved at my mom, "Hi, Mrs. Harper," and rushed over to me. She bent close and asked, "Hey, Laurie with an L, everything okay?"

I just shook my head.

"Your house a little *different*?"

I nodded, silently.

Jenny Withajay clapped her hands. "It worked! You remembered!"

I could tell she knew what was going on, although I would never have guessed that she was the cause. I whispered, "What worked?"

But she said, "Hey, Mrs. Harper, how are things?"

"Fine, Jenny."

"Everything normal?"

"Of course, dear. What are you on about now?"

Jenny giggled. "Oh, nothing. Just making maps."

And that's how it started.

At first I didn't believe that Jenny was the cause.

I figured she was lying.

Normally I let Jenny's lies play themselves out. Okay, maybe it's not fair to call them lies. I know she believes many of them. If something is false but you believe it, are you lying when you tell it to someone else? Some things, though, Jenny knows aren't true, yet she goes on and on about them, as if she's on a stage and performing stories that *should* be true. She's obviously performing, however, and even though she won't admit she's lying, you know she is, and she knows you know, and you're both in silent agreement that she's full of crap and so you let it slide.

This time, though, I was in no mood to let it slide. I told her to tell me the truth. Hurt, she said that *was* the truth. I told her it was *not*. We went back and forth like that for a while. Before things got really ugly between us, she proved it to me. Right in front of me she dismapped our street, drawing it quickly on a scrap of paper, making it wider and straighter and renaming it *Esmeralda Avenue* (after her favorite old stuffed bear), and sure enough, when we went outside, I looked at the street and its sign and saw that we now lived on straight and wide Esmeralda Avenue.

I was frightened by Jenny's little act of power. She was merely tickled by it. She said it was nothing, really. She'd done *way* much more already. After dismapping her house and my house, she had dismapped Greenland right out of existence. She had never liked Greenland because, on almost any map, it wasn't shaped right, it was always deceptive, way up there in the Arctic and looking much bigger than it really was. So she mapped the North Atlantic—from Baffin Island across to Norway—without a Greenland in it. Greenland is *gone,* now, gone from the North Atlantic, gone from the globe in my brother's room, gone from our social studies books, gone from the dictionary and the encyclopedia, gone from every memory but mine and Jenny Withajay's.

I asked Jenny about all the people who had lived in Greenland.

"Oh, don't worry," she said. "I scattered all the cities in other countries. Holsteinsborg is next to Philadelphia and

Angmagssalik is next to Tokyo and Ivigtut is next to Nairobi. I forget where I put all the rest."

"Yeah, but what about the people who weren't living in the cities?"

She shrugged. "They must still be in Greenland."

"But Greenland's *gone*."

She got angry. "What, you think I *killed* everyone? You think I didn't think of this? I renamed the rest of Greenland and put it in Brazil, right on the equator where it'll never be misshapen again. See?" She pulled out one of her atlases and showed me. She flipped through the pages, found South America, and pointed to a tiny place called Whiteland.

I guess I was relieved.

Jenny's been at it again.

I was watching the weather channel today. Sometimes it's the quickest way to find out what Jenny has done. Otherwise I have to flip through an atlas to see what's changed. I certainly can't ask my family or anyone else about it, since they don't know any better.

Anyhow, today Jenny moved Egypt into Canada.

There weren't any special news reports about the sudden relocation of Egypt. As far as everyone else is concerned, Egypt has always been in the middle of Canada. It isn't news. But just as a matter of course, the weather channel reported on the weather in Canada, and as if nothing's amiss the weather guy says, "This storm'll drop a quarter inch of rain on Edmonton before passing into Cairo."

So there it is. Egypt has found a new home. Now, in an afternoon, you can take a canoe ride up the Nile River to Beaverhill Lake. You can play hockey between the pyramids.

That isn't the end of it, either. Germany is now a string of islands in the Pacific. Italy isn't shaped like a boot anymore; it's shaped like a hand. And Michigan, which used to be shaped like a hand, is now shaped like a head. Jenny put a gigantic lake where Kansas used to be and she stuck Kansas between Mongolia and China. She took all the nations of Africa, made them square, and lined them up neatly. She took Hollywood out of California and put it on the edge of Antarctica. They don't make as many movies as they used to.

Nothing's the same, and I'm sure that tomorrow Jenny will get bored with what she's done and she'll dismap it all again. I have no idea what she'll dismap, exactly. I don't know her plans. I really don't know what she's up to. I could ask her but that wouldn't do me any good. Jenny will do what Jenny will do, whether I'm informed or not.

Jenny has refused to fix my house, to put it back the way it was. At least no rooms are missing. But have you ever realized how much of your house is a *habit*? You don't even *think* about it. You just *know*. But now I *have* to think about it. Otherwise I'll run into a wall. And I wonder, Will this wall be here tomorrow? Will it be here the next time I pass it? Every time I take a step I expect it all to change again. My house just isn't trustworthy anymore. It's a little scary when you can't trust your own house.

Of course it's not really my *house* I can't trust.

I suppose I should be grateful I didn't live in Angmagssalik. Oh, sure, maybe the rest of the world's getting it worse than me. Jenny's not just moving cities and countries: She's uprooting people. I wonder how many *families* Jenny has dismapped. Just imagine! There's some mother still in San Diego, but her grown-up son in Hollywood is now at the bottom of the world. Even if he's forgotten *where* he used to be, has he forgotten *who* he used to be?

I can only hope he *has* forgotten.

I wish *I* could forget the way the world was. I mean, this is driving me *nuts*. You know I'm about to flunk history? I can't keep up. Every time Jenny dismaps a country, she dismaps the past. After all, where you live is where you *do*, do everything, I mean, like building and fighting and all of it. It's actually a little creepy—no, a *lot* creepy—how history settles down to fit Jenny's latest geography. There are wars that I never heard of, kings that I never heard of, whole *eras* with big fat important-sounding names that I never *ever* heard of. I used to study history once a week—I'd do it all at once so it made some sense—but now I'm cramming all the time. And it won't do any good. I know I'm going to flunk.

That, I guess, is the least of my problems. Next up is my house, but I've mentioned that already. Then there's my neighborhood.

I admit it's not hard to get used to a street named Esmeralda, but Jenny has also rearranged and even *removed* some other streets nearby. She got rid of Orangelawn, which is where the Mitchells lived, and that's no great loss, since Donna Mitchell was a *pain* and so were all her brothers (and who cares where they are now)—but I used to take Orange-lawn to the Tel-Six mall and now I have to take Fenton. I don't like Fenton because Bobby lives there and, oh, I like *Bobby* but walking past *his* house would make me *way* too self-conscious—and who needs that? Yeah, I could take Revere and I suppose I will, but that's so roundabout, espe-cially now that Jenny has made Revere a winding road. Maybe, in the end, I'll simply cut through some yards.

Okay, okay. I can *live* with it.

But do you know what it's like to hear your friends say, "See you at the Tel-Six!"—and then you realize you don't know where the Tel-Six *is* anymore? I couldn't *find* it. Jenny hadn't just eliminated Orangelawn; she had moved the Tel-Six be-hind the HomeBuilders Warehouse. You couldn't even see it from the street. Sure, I finally figured out where it was, but *I had to figure it out.* Everyone else was already waiting at Pizza Joe's. They didn't care that I was late, they just thought I was delayed, but in fact I was *lost.* I felt so small and annoyed. I wasn't very good company.

I went to Jenny later and asked her what *else* she had messed up. She said she hadn't "messed up" anything. I told her about the Tel-Six and she said, "It's still there, isn't it?"

"But why didn't you *tell* me?" I cried.

"What for?" she said. "I'm not even sure I'm keeping it there. I only put it there at lunchtime. I might put it out by the Crossing instead."

"But the trains are a mile away!"

"So?"

"So I don't want to *walk* a *mile* to the mall!"

"It's just the Tel-Six. There are better stores at White Oaks. Hey! I'll put White Oaks at the end of Esmeralda. Right where the bus stops. Cool!"

I told her not to.

She stared at me. She *glared* at me. I had already complained when she refused to fix my house. She had been so *obnoxious,* then. She acted as if my complaints weren't important, as if *nothing* were so important as Jenny Withajay's Absolute Right to Dismap Everything and Leave It Dismapped. I had bit my lip, then, and let it slide. But now I wasn't merely complaining—I was *commanding*—and it was quite obvious I didn't approve of Jenny's dismapping. She glared at me with a glare a mile deep and said, "Laurie with an L, you are *not* my mother."

Then, right in front of me, she scribbled the Tel-Six by the Crossing and scrawled White Oaks at the end of our street.

I called her a name and left.

Maybe I lost my temper too quickly. But think about it. Jenny moves the Tel-Six behind the Warehouse. She doesn't tell me she did. Not the end of the world, no. But when I ask her *why* she didn't tell me, she says, "What for?" As if there's *no reason* to tell me. As if *I don't matter.* Here I am, the only person who's getting confused by Jenny's dismapping, and *she doesn't care.* Heck, she rubs my face in it. To spite me she moves the Tel-Six *again*, to the Crossing—she does precisely what I told her not to.

Tough luck, Laurie with an L!

How could she *do* that to me?

I would never have said that Jenny was kind or thoughtful. Yes, she has *always* been a little selfish. But it's always been a kind of *carelessness*. There was never anything *nasty* about it. She just did things and, well, if they hurt somebody, well, okay, then she'd stop. She'd never apologize, she'd never try to make amends, but at least she'd *stop*.

So that was it. I wasn't going to wait until this thing became a crisis.

If Jenny wouldn't stop it, then I would.

It became a crisis.

We'd had our fight about the Tel-Six soon after dinner. I went home in a crummy mood, did my homework in a crummy mood, watched TV in an utterly crummy mood, and then, even though it was almost nine, I decided I had to stop Jenny Withajay. I didn't know *how*, but I would do it.

I told my mom I was going to see Jenny. She said it was too late to go visiting. I said it wasn't *that* late, it wasn't even dark yet, and she said, "Well, at least get back before the second sun sets."

The *second* sun?

I didn't ask her what she meant. I could tell she meant exactly what she said. I went outside unhappily. I didn't want to see it but I saw it. I looked up, shielding my eyes, and, sure enough, there was the yellow sun, the old familiar sun, setting towards the housetops—and up to its left, higher in the sky, was a bright little blue sun. I had two shadows.

"Oh, no," I sighed. Jenny was dismapping the solar system now.

Then I noticed, off to the south, a huge *something* above the horizon. It was more or less flat, maybe a mile thick, and miles across. It was moving, floating. I squinted at it, focusing on it, and I swear I saw buildings. *Cities*. Trees, mountains. I knew what it was. The only thing it *could* be. It was a country, some country, a small country, sure, but all of it was up in the sky. Off to the east, in the haze, was another one. I had no idea how Jenny had done it—layers of paper?—but now she was dismapping in three dimensions.

She had been awfully busy in the past couple of hours.

And then when I'm a little more than halfway to her house, there's a quake like a towel snap, an instant and terrible crack of the earth and a shudder in the ground, a wind that slaps my back and hits my face, and then, just as suddenly, it's as quiet a September evening as ever there was.

In front of me everything was normal—except, of course, for the floating countries and the double shadows. I turned around.

Behind me was a hole . . . no, a *gap*. Right across the neighborhood. I walked over to it slowly, afraid the ground might crack again and swallow me. There was a high fence but I could see into the gap. I couldn't see the bottom. The other side was easily a mile away. The gap went endlessly to the right and endlessly to the left. On the fence there was a sign. It told me the name of this tremendous canyon.

It was the same name I had called Jenny.

The sign also said this was MILE 0 of the canyon. I glanced across the street. There was another sign. I ran to it. This sign said MILE 24,855.

The canyon went all the way around the world.

Oh, I could tell *exactly* what Jenny had done.

Madder than ever I ran the rest of the way to her house.

"You split us up!" I yelled.

Jenny was surprised to see me. For a moment she was irritated. Then, as I stood on her front porch, separated from her by the screen door, she became almost indifferent. She said, "Whatever do you mean?"

"You cut the world in half! Between my house and yours." Suddenly a terrible thought occurred to me. "My house! The canyon goes right—"

She snorted. "Your house is fine. It's on the other side."

"Which is where you wanted *me*, right?"

She shrugged.

"Lucky *you*," I said. "I was on my way here, on *your* side."

"I knew I should have done it hours ago."

"So why *didn't* you?"

She shrugged. "I wasn't mad enough."

"And now you are?"

She shrugged again.

I tried to be calm. "Look, Jenny. Let me in."

"No."

"Then come out here."

She scowled.

I took a breath. "You're being a baby."

"More name-calling, huh?"

"Oh, come on. What are you, made of jelly? Grow up."

Her arms were at her sides. She made fists of both her hands. "Watch it. I might just dismap *you*."

"What?"

"You think I can't?" She grinned. "A nose is just a mountain, an eye's a lake, a mouth's a road, an ear's a little building, and a cheek's a vacant lot. I know I could never *draw* your face—but I *could* dismap it. My dismaps are just *scribbles,* Laurie with an L. They're not drawings. All I have to do is *scribble* something on a piece of paper, and tons of rocks and bricks and people *move*." She suddenly opened the door, almost hitting me with it, and stepped out on the porch. She waved at the suns. "You see it! *Two* of them. I made another *sun*. All I did was draw two circles with squiggly rays and color one of them blue. That's *it*. All that matters is what I *want*." She crossed her arms and stared at me. "Maybe I want you *mutant ugly*."

I crossed my arms, too. "I don't want *you* mutant ugly."

"Ha! You can't *make* me."

"Even if I could, I wouldn't."

She glared at me.

"Jenny." I sighed. "You know you're making me mad. You usually do. But I've never *hated* you before. Do you hate me, now?"

The look on her face was so odd. It was as if my question were a blast of air across a candle flame. Some fire was suddenly gone and Jenny was as calm as curling smoke. She looked down.

"Do you?" I asked again.

"No."

"Then quit acting like you do."

She snarled, "Don't order me. You're not my mother."

"That's right. I'm your *friend*."

It was the mushiest thing I had ever said.

She looked up. After a moment, she sighed. "Okay, okay. I'm sorry I split the world. I'll put it back, okay?"

"And the rest of it."

"Huh?"

"All of it. Put it all back."

Maybe I was pushing too much too quickly, but I had to say it.

She shook her head. "No. It's too cool. I like it."

"It's all *wrong*, though."

"It's all *different*. And so what? Everything changes sooner or later."

"Yeah, but it's not your job to change it."

"Why not?"

"It just isn't."

"Whatever. I still like my dismaps."

"But they're not *true*, Jenny."

"So?" She laughed. "Lots of things aren't."

"Not your maps. A map that isn't true isn't any good."

She looked away.

I uncrossed my arms. "Put everything back, Jenny. Please." That's all I asked. I didn't ask for an apology. I didn't expect Jenny to apologize to me. She never apologizes. So maybe it's *not* like she stole my boyfriend or spread nasty rumors about me. It was still bad, you know? She put a bottomless pit between us. That *hurt*. Even so, I didn't ask for any apology. I only wanted her to dismap her dismaps. I only asked for everything normal.

She scowled so tightly, then, as if she were shutting her head. I swear her scowl worked its way through all her bones. Finally she cried, "All *right*, already. I'll put it *all* back." She grabbed at the screen door and swung it open, almost hitting me again, and shot back into her house. She slammed the front door without saying another thing to me.

"Jenny!" I shouted.

I thought about banging on the door, but I knew it wouldn't do much apart from bothering Jenny's mom and dad. Jenny wasn't coming back to *that* door, not for a while. Okay, fine. So we were ignoring each other for now. Fine. It's happened before. At least *this* was normal. It was better than the Jenny who made stars and cracked worlds. I shrugged and turned to go home. Of course, then I remembered that I wasn't very good at leaping over mile-wide gaps in the ground.

So I sat on Jenny's steps, elbows on my knees and chin in my hands, hoping that she'd remove the canyon before the suns set.

"SHE CHECKS MY SPINE FOR THE BOPPER ROOTS AND THERE THEY
ARE, ALL TEN TRILLION OF THEM, VIOLET ORANGE AND GLOWING
UNDER MY SKIN, AS NORMAL AND HEALTHY AS EVER."

WALK THIS WAY

She's the only Mae in our school. She's the only Mae I know. She's the only Mae I've ever heard of. I say *Mae* and I know who I mean. There's only one Mae I can mean. There's only one Mae.

I could write her a poem but I don't know how. I'm not a poet. I don't like poetry. Poetry's just a mess, to me. A poem is like a story that can't make up its mind and spins around and falls down and shatters. Just a mess. But I know that love causes a lot of poetry so I'm thinking I should write Mae a poem. I wouldn't know what to write, though. I already said I'm not a poet.

I just like Mae an awful lot.

So what can I do?

Watch her when she walks.

Mae walks. I don't just mean from her couch to her kitchen. I mean from *everywhere* to *everywhere*. To the mall, to our school, to her friends. Of course she can only get into places with doors, but most places still have doors, you know. I'm sure you don't use them any more than I do but next time you bop somewhere, look around. There's more doors than you'd think. There's even lots of sidewalks left. And that's where Mae goes. On sidewalks and through doors.

When I finally do talk to her, I mean for real, like personal, the poetry kind of talk, I'm going to ask her if she can even bop at all. It's a rude question, I know, but someday we'll be in a personal, poetic kind of way and then it won't be rude. For now I like to think she can but won't. If she *can't,* that would mean that maybe she's sick. That would make me sad. I don't want Mae to be sick. I don't think she *is* sick. I've seen people who can't bop. It's usually obvious, too, just like people who can't walk or see or hear or talk. You can just tell. But not with Mae. She just walks, that's all. Except for the fact that she's Mae, she's obviously like anyone else.

I'm trying not to bop as much.

I figure if Mae and I grow up together, like forever, and even end up married, I'm going to have to get used to walking a lot. It's tough not to bop. I'm so used to just thinking, "Well, I think I'll go get a burger," and *bop!* I'm there, and the only feet-moving I do is while my line creeps up to the counter. Then I buy my food and by then my bopper's warmed back up and *bop!* I'm home again. I've got a pretty healthy bopper, too. I'm still a kid, after all, not some worn-out old guy, and I eat right (sort of) and I exercise (well, I kick a lot of soccer balls). Maybe sometimes I've pushed my bopper too hard. Haven't you ever tried to bop as fast as possible? I've dare-bopped with my friend Eric and gone down to only fifty-six seconds between bops. We timed it. Not the world's record, but even so. Eric never got below a minute. Of course he *can* belch for thirty-seven seconds. We timed it.

My family is thinking the usual family-worries about me. I tell my mom I just don't *want* to bop. She puts the back of her hand against my forehead anyhow and swears I'm feverish. But I'm not. Then she watches how much I eat. Same stuff I always eat and just as much. I bopped across the room just to prove I'm fine. She makes me take off my shirt anyhow. She checks my spine for the bopper roots and there they are, all ten trillion of them, violet orange and glowing under my skin, as normal and healthy as ever.

Then my dad asks me if I'm taking sludgers. I know he's worried but does he think I'm stupid? I've had all those classes at school where they warn us about sludging. They told us to stay away from anyone who sells sludgers. Mom and Dad have been telling me the same thing for years. To be honest I don't know why anyone would take a sludger on purpose. Why stifle your bopper with a pill? Only uncontrollable kids and guys in jail get fed sludgers.

Then my sister thinks I'm hanging out with some bunch of attitude kids, the kind of kids who rip their pants and pierce their noses and talk back to grown-ups and won't do anything normal. Bopping is too normal for some kids. It's hard to put out your I'm-too-cool-for-it-all attitude when you're bopping as much as any smiling granny. So there are kids in my school who make a point of not bopping. They decorate their shoes with splatter paint and flashy buckles and neon laces and step loudly so you know they're not bopping. There might be kids like that at your school. I'm certainly not one of them. I told my sister I never could be. I don't think she believed me but then I don't think she ever believes me.

Then my brother says, "There's only one thing ever makes a guy do irrational things. It's gotta be a girl." Dad says, "What, now a guy has to stop bopping to get a girl's attention?" They all think about that, like it's far too weird. Then my sister jumps up and cries, "I know why! It's *Mae,* I've seen him watching her, he's in love with *Mae,* she never bops and so he's acting like her because *he loves Mae!*" The look on my face gives it all away. Everyone knows my sister's snagged the truth. Mom stares at me like there's something not quite right about me anymore. My brother says, "Told ya. I *knew* it. A girl! Man, he'd be better off sick."

Mae's not an attitude kid. Her shoes aren't splatter and neon. They're just shoes that cover her feet. And she doesn't step loudly. In fact it's almost like she's skating and the blades never quite leave the ice. She walks like she has to help gravity keep her from floating away. She's as fast as a skater but also just as connected to the ground. It's a busy but graceful way of walking.

For me it would be running.

I wonder if she's making up for not bopping. If you want to

walk, then walk fast. And that makes me wonder, again, if she *wants* to walk. I like to *think* she has a choice, but maybe, in the end, she doesn't. She might not even *have* a bopper. She might have been born without one. Or what almost happened to my uncle may have happened to her. He went into the hospital to get his right leg fixed but every document said it was his *left* leg that needed fixing, and no matter what my aunt said to the nurses and doctors, the documents always said *left*. She finally took a black marker and wrote WRONG ONE on his left leg, so the surgeon wouldn't make a mistake. Maybe Mae went in for a tonsillectomy and accidentally got a bopperectomy.

She may have her bopper after all but it might not work. Or her bopper may work and she may be the farthest thing from sick, but she just never got to Neither-Nor. It could happen. Lots of kids never learn to ride a bike, either, or learn to swim. It took *me* a year to get to Neither-Nor. I was over eleven. I was almost twelve before I got to Or. My bop teacher, Mrs. Firth, told me over and over, "You are here. You want to be there. You have two possibilities. Here. There. *Either* here *or* there. Right now you are here. You are *Either*. You want to be there. You want to be *Or*. The only way you can pass from *Either* to *Or* is to become *Neither-Nor*. You have to be *neither* here *nor* there. Then stop being *Neither-Nor*, but instead of falling back to *Either*, fall forward to *Or*. Then you are there instead of here."

That, of course, was not so helpful. It's like telling a kid, "If you want to stay balanced on a bike, just don't tip over." But normally Mrs. Firth didn't spend so much time trying to explain things. You learn to bop by doing exercises, not by thinking, but with me she could get kind of desperate. She figured she had to make me *understand*, since I was having such a hard time *doing*. Maybe it worked after all. I can bop, anyhow.

It could be that Mae never had a Mrs. Firth to help her. We might all be born with boppers, but bopping isn't natural. You know somebody has to teach you. So it's like nobody ever taught Mae. She never had a bopping exercise. A part of everybody else's life was never a part of hers. It's like Mae is dirt poor or something.

I hate to say it, but that's kind of romantic, isn't it? In a tragic, poetic kind of way.

Mrs. Firth used to say that bopping is all about *possibilities*. If a bop is possible, then you can bop. You've probably heard that a null-bop grid is like a shield. Well, it isn't. If you try to bop to a place inside a null-bop grid, it's not like you're bounced back. You never even go. It's just *not possible* for you to bop inside a null-bop grid, so there's no *there* to go to. You don't start with an *Either here or there*. There's no possibility of the *Or there*. All you have is the *Either here*. That's it. So *here* you stay.

It's all very strange.

Some of our neighbors wanted to get together and lay a null-bop grid throughout the neighborhood (to keep out any bopping trespassers), but they couldn't raise enough money. On top of that, the utilities commission wouldn't zone us for a grid. And some of our other neighbors were afraid that the grid would mess with their brains. You know how it is. A grid puts out an awful magnetic field.

There are other ways of making bops impossible. Sludgers, of course. Or bopperectomies. But people don't appreciate being drugged up or cut up.

Besides, people *want* to bop. So what if it causes trouble? You know how people used to get around in cars? Every year, fifty thousand people *died* in car accidents. I didn't believe that number either, but I looked it up. Fifty thousand a year. Just in our country. And people kept driving cars.

Here's an easy question. WHAT MUST YOU NEVER DO? Unless your parents are brain dead, they must have told you twenty bazillion times, NEVER BOP TO A PRIVATE PLACE. If there's no grid, that's the best you can do. You can't force people to take sludgers or get bopperectomies, unless they actually get caught doing bad things. And the boppers aren't going away. Every normal newborn baby has a bopper. The bopper virus settled in a long time ago.

The best you can do is hope that people are good.

It's hard to be good.

I know what the law is. I know what's right. But you know how often I've wanted to bop right next to Mae? It sometimes seems like that's the only way I can get close to her. It'd be easier than trying to *talk* to her. I bet, though, that I'd crash right into her. My atoms would probably get mixed up with hers.

Okay, I know that can't happen. It isn't *possible* to mix atoms like that. Two people can't be in the same place at the same time. You just can't bop to an impossible place.

♦ ♦ ♦

This afternoon I talked to Mae. For real.

I was watching her walk, as usual. She was on her way home from school. Our school building is old and all the doors still work. Mae left by the front door. By herself. I was watching her from Mr. Kerry's classroom. I sometimes help Mr. Kerry sort papers and stuff. The window was open, because the day had been nice, although it had rained a little, and there were raindrops trapped in the cross-hatching of the screen. I could smell the damp dust on the sill. I heard the water two floors above me, dripping from the gutters.

Soon she was too far away. I knew I shouldn't but I decided to bop to where she was. I really wanted to talk to her. I didn't *expect* to talk to her, but I certainly couldn't talk to her from Mr. Kerry's room. Even after I bopped, I would probably stay in hiding, but you never know.

I bopped to some hedges nearby. I crouched down. The rain had thrown little twigs all over the ground. The sides of the trees were wet.

Mae was gone.

Where was she? I had just seen her! For a second I thought I had been stuck in Neither-Nor. They say that you're only in Neither-Nor for less than an instant, and that's all it ever seems to be, but you know how everyone's a little afraid of being stuck there for longer than that. It could be days since I bopped. Years, even. I might still be a kid, but Mae could be a *grandma* by now.

Then I heard her from right behind me. She said, "Hello."

She said it in a *Boo*-voice, trying to scare me, and she scared me pretty good. She startled me right into the hedge. I got scratched by the thorns. I turned around as guilty as could be. She had this smile like she had won some little game. In a way she had. She had caught me and I didn't even know I was being chased.

"You know," she said, "you're being kind of rude."

This was not the way I had wanted to talk to her. This wasn't just some chatter during class. This wasn't just saying hi in the hall. But it also wasn't poetry. It was just embarrassing.

I shrugged. "Sorry. I didn't mean anything."

She stopped smiling. "Yes, you *did.* Your sister says you do."

My sister! That *creep.*

Mae looked aside, almost away. "If you want to walk with me, I don't care. But don't bop and hide. Okay?"

"Okay."

She nodded, then smiled again. She walked away.

I caught up with her and for a little while I just tried to keep up. I tried very hard to pretend we were just walking. Like it was no big deal. I think I was happy. I wasn't sure at the time. But things were good.

Almost poetry.

"Mae?"

"Yeah?"

"Don't your feet ever get tired?"

"Nope. Not my legs, either."

Then I just had to ask.

"Mae, don't you like bopping?"

"I don't hate it."

"So you *can* bop?"

"Of course I can bop." She stopped. "You want to see?"

"That's okay. I know what bopping looks like."

She put out her hand. "Come on. I'll show you." I didn't put out my own hand, but not because I didn't want to. "Come on. I don't have the plague." I stared at her. Now she was getting a little uncomfortable, too. Whatever my sister had said to Mae, it had made Mae kind of brave, brave enough to hold hands with me. But now I was acting like maybe I didn't like Mae, not *that* much, not yet. But I *did* like her that much. Before she started feeling foolish, I took her hand. She seemed relieved.

Then she bopped.

We didn't go far. At first I didn't think we went anywhere. It was the same scenery. Then I realized we were five feet in the air.

And we weren't falling.

I wanted to grab hold of something but there was only Mae to hold. Luckily we were still holding hands. And I didn't feel any weight at all. I gaped at her. I was so shocked I wasn't even able to ask her *how*, but she could tell I wanted to ask.

She said, "I can bop constantly. All we're doing is bopping to the same place over and over again, so fast that gravity can't get a good hold of us. We're not exactly floating. We're here, then we're not, then we are."

"But your bopper!"

"What about it?"

"How does it warm up so fast?"

She shrugged. "I don't know. It's always warmed up."

I looked around us. We were really, truly *not falling*. "This is *wild*, Mae. Were you *born* like this?"

"I guess so."

I looked at the ground. "Can your parents do it, too?"

"Nope. Just me. I'm the only bird in the family."

I looked back at her. "Bird?"

"Sure. If I bopped a smidgen higher, then another smidgen, then another smidgen, again and again, I'd be flying."

"You can *fly*?"

"As good as."

"So why do you *walk*?"

She smiled. "I *like* to walk."

I told you I liked Mae an awful lot. I still do, even more so. It turns out that Mae likes me, too, more than I could have hoped.

We walk together almost every day.

And sometimes we fly.

"I HEARD HIS PAINT-THOUGHTS AND FELT THEM PASS TO
WALLS AND CLOTHES AND CHATTERBOOKS."

POOF POOF YA DOES ME A FAVOR

Poof Poof Ya is really Dexter Rigato and every kid in school knows it. He keeps it a secret only from the adults. The kids keep it a secret, too, among themselves. What adult would believe them anyhow? And in any event, Poof Poof Ya is just a vandal to the adults. They have no idea that he's using his *mind* to do what he does. For the adults, Poof Poof Ya is just another kid with a can of spray paint, going about and defacing the school; just another delinquent and not any sort of phenomenon.

But Dexter doesn't spray *paint*. He sprays *thoughts.*

Poof poof ya was the very first thing that Dexter *deliberately* painted on a wall, the outside wall at the back of the gym. It was not, however, his *first* paint-thought. His first paint-thoughts had been random and involuntary, no better than brain sneezes, the likes of *ouch, ick,* and *aaagh;* yet when he gained control of his paint-thinking and went out to use it, he couldn't think of anything to paint and he was too impatient to bother thinking of anything. In his excitement he painted *poof poof ya.*

Just another brain sneeze.

But Dexter enjoyed the sound of it. He painted *poof poof ya* over and over, on walls and floors and ceilings throughout the school. That's how he got his alias, and his fame. He never hid his power from his friends. He told his tale to any fan. And although Dexter tells all, not even his enemies have betrayed the secret of Poof Poof Ya, for as was said, no one would believe them; and besides, Dexter let it be known that if Poof Poof Ya were ever betrayed, the betrayers would suffer some terrible telepathic torture.

In truth, Dexter could never telepathically torture anyone, but no one has been inclined to call his bluff.

There are still a few kids who doubt that he paint-thinks, even after they've seen him do it. There is one kid, however, who knows without a doubt that Dexter's power is real. Her name is Meredith Simmons. She, too, has an unusual mind: She talks to the planet Pluto—their souls have been entangled since her conception. However Dexter's doing what he does, he's doing it through the same spaces that entangle Meredith and Pluto. Whenever Dexter paints, Meredith can hear his thoughts.

I tell Pluto I live on Earth, that I am *not* Earth but a girl living *on* Earth, and even now, after we've been entangled for over fourteen years, I don't think he entirely believes me.

That's not so surprising. He still thinks he's the only planet in the universe. Why should he believe in girls when he doesn't quite believe in Earth?

I explain that there are nine planets and he is the ninth. I remind him of his moon, Charon, and ask him to imagine things like Charon, like himself, circling the sun. He does believe in Charon. Charon he feels. And the sun he feels. But he calls Charon his Cold-Me. He calls the sun his Warm-Me. In his mind, another Cold-Me circling his Warm-Me would still be himself. He says that if Earth is real, then it is just his Dark-Me.

To Pluto, everything is Me.

I am his Other-Me.

Sometimes, depending on his mood (and on mine), I am his Loud-Me, his Pest-Me, his Song-Me, his Fun-Me, his Dear-Me, his Confusing-Me. I don't stay one kind of Me. What's more, I actually *talk* to Pluto. Sometimes I talk back. I'm not merely cold like Charon or warm like the sun. I'm a girl, after all, not a heavenly body, and after several billion years of simple Me-ness, Pluto sometimes has a hard time dealing with simple me.

Dexter hasn't become popular in any normal sense. He's not suddenly invited to parties, he's not running for student council, he's not hanging with the celebrity kids. He's more like the Grand Canyon. Kids come to see him, and just like acres of desert chasms, he causes awe.

And in the cafeteria, at the table he has claimed as his

court, he grandly tells of his being Poof Poof Ya. Today, for example, he says, "Yeah, I could go other places if I *wanted*, but what *for*? Nah. Everyone knows me here. This is *my* school. Right, I could go to Holmes and *then* what? Spray *their* walls and tell them it was Poof Poof Ya and his *MINDPAINT* and get *beat* up or something for being some sort of *liar* from Winston. Who needs *that*? Nah. *Maybe* when I get better at this I'll *go* spray all of Mt. Rushmore or whatever. I'd have to *get* there, though. At least I *think* I would. I'll tell you a secret—I've never sprayed long-distance. I will, though, when the time is right. But Mt. Rushmore? Nah. I'd be bugging people I *don't know*. And *here* I get to bug Mr. Cheesehead. The guy wants *so bad* to find Poof Poof Ya and there *I* go, walking past his office *every* day. He never sees *me* with a can of paint. *That's* what's fun."

Mr. Cheesehead is the principal. His real name is Chezznik.

Now, Dexter speaks as though he's sharing some example of careful logic, but he's only rambling. He always rambles. No one complains. In the end he doesn't demand to be treated as logical or any such thing. He simply likes being famous and talking about himself.

I'm not sure how I realized that he is Pluto. When my father read me a picture book about the solar system, it simply *hit* me. I suddenly *knew* that *my* Other-Me was in fact a planet.

I got used to that fact rather quickly, more quickly than perhaps I should have. I thought that mind-talking with planets was just a part of being alive. Pluto's slow, large voice has always been at the back of my mind. I can spend hours doing this or that, waiting for him to finish speaking. He's as natural to me as my heartbeat. Only when I was four or so did I realize how abnormal it actually was, when I recognized how much it bewildered and worried my parents, and I learned not to mention my friend the planet Pluto. Then I thought I was unique. Not *purely* unique, of course. I may talk to a planet—but there's a planet that talks to me. One could say that Pluto's mind is precisely as abnormal as mine. In fact I *do* say that, whenever he starts in on how strange *I* am.

It was when I learned to talk that Pluto realized something truly wasn't right about his Other-Me. Before then I had seemed like a weird dream to him. But then I spoke, and spoke to him, and said things he didn't expect. I said things he didn't understand. In fact his ideas about pests and songs and the like all come from me, his Strange-Me, since before me he had never had to come up with the *idea* of a pest or the *idea* of a song.

No pests or songs where Pluto lives.

I have filled his life with ideas because my life has streamed into him. It isn't always clear to him, but he knows what I feel, what I think, what I say. He knows what I *do*—and everything I've done: tying my shoes, crawling up stairs, dressing my dolls, swimming in ponds, staring at boys, drawing with crayons, hugging my father, riding my bike, going to dances, kneeling in church, sleeping in my mother's arms. Pluto doesn't entirely understand *doing* but

I am so rich with it that he almost envies it. After all, he doesn't *do* much of anything. He has nothing to do.

Whenever an adult comes near, Dexter changes the subject. He *is* a vandal, after all. He has to hide his tale from those who would cut it off. But at the moment there are only kids, so Dexter rambles on.

Today, Meredith is in his audience.

His audience is not very large. The kids try to police themselves and keep the crowds small around Dexter. No one wants to attract too much attention. Everyone gets a chance to see him, though, sooner or later. This is Meredith's third time.

Dexter announces that he's ready to sell something. He puts out his hand and the girl nearest him gives him a dollar and a chatterbook. Her chatterbook is not some little hardbound diary, as many are, but just a few sheets of looseleaf folded and stapled together. Dexter has never objected to painting on mere looseleaf. He paints on anything—even clothes and faces. (Not always permanently: Mindpaint, like any paint, can be washed off of *some* things.) It has become the fashion, however, to collect bits of Poof Poof Ya's chatter not on fabrics and skin, but in little books. This girl's book already has some of his chatter in it. Meredith can see the bright mindpaint on the paper.

Dexter is more or less generous. He'll sell chatter for as little as a dime, but of course one gets what one pays for. For a dollar, Poof Poof Ya will chatter four words. His choice. For a higher, negotiated fee, he will chatter whatever he is told. He is even available for hire as an untouchable vandal. After all, why risk one's *own* neck spray-painting J. T. LOVES L. C. on some overpass, when Poof Poof Ya will do it risk free?

Dexter pockets the dollar and opens the chatterbook to a blank page. His fame, like any fame, depends on *displaying* his power. He makes sure that everyone sees. He doesn't wave his hands or flutter his fingers, like some magician; but of course magicians do that only to distract people. Magicians are fakes. Poof Poof Ya is real. Dexter simply lays the page in front of himself and paints it.

He does add a *little* drama. The chatter doesn't appear all at once. One letter may trace itself, cursively, and another assemble itself from random splatters, and another roll into sight, as if from a printing press. He's done it a hundred times before, but it never ceases to awe his audience. Today, for the girl, Poof Poof Ya vividly delivers a dollar's worth of vivid chatter.

Four words, straight from his thoughts.

Then a fifth.

The fifth word appears suddenly, whole, colorful, complete in a flash, much like Dexter's earlier brain sneezes; and like a sneeze, it doesn't seem to mean anything. Dexter is confused. He did *not* think this word—yet there it is, painted by him. He has the wit, however, not to *look* confused. Before anyone can think he can't count to four or, worse, that he's lost control, he says, "And *there,* an extra word just because I'm in the mood."

Everyone is pretty much pleased by this generous stunt. Meredith is pleased, too, but only because the word is hers.

◆ ◆ ◆

Sometimes I get tired of Pluto. I get tired of explaining that I'm a girl. By now I've said it a million times. Like a frozen river his mind cracks a little, and churns below itself, and there's the smallest thaw as some bit of him pushes against another, but whatever rises usually sinks again. No matter how much of my life he shares, he can never truly understand the most important thing about being a girl: A girl is not Pluto. I even speak as slowly as he speaks—to explain as slowly as I can—but it does no good. I slow my thoughts so much that they nearly become wordless, as they were when I was a baby. As a matter of fact Pluto misses my baby thoughts and, even more so, my thoughts *before* I was born, when I was a kind of Pluto myself, alone inside my mother. My thoughts then were never slow, but to Pluto they were sweet and much less troublesome.

Sometimes he gets tired of me. He even wishes I would go away. He never hates me. I never hate him. How could we hate each other? But he's not always so fond of me. We clash because he can't accept that his Other-Me isn't him. I insist, year after year, but he's so stubborn. I guess I should be more patient with him. He's had aeons to get used to himself and not even fifteen years to get used to me. But it's so *frustrating*.

I am *not* Pluto.

I know we are not the same person. I know I have my own mind. I've got a head and a brain inside and I feel my own soul at work. And I know that Pluto is *not* some little knot in myself. I admit it doesn't make sense that a planet could think. Maybe they *all* do, maybe it's perfectly normal, but it doesn't make sense and, in any event, I've never heard any others. Pluto's alone. How could one mind be so utterly alone? Only God was ever so alone. Pluto's obviously not God, though.

So why has God given Pluto a soul at all, only to put him out at the far, cold edge of everything? He's a cold rock orbited by a cold rock. He may call the sun his Warm-Me, but that's only because he knows no better. The sun's warmth is actually meager where he lives. I try to explain to him that the sun is *hot,* so very hot, but I might as well be trying to explain Heaven.

I just drown in his icy waters.

As lunch ends and the audience leaves, Meredith lingers.

Meredith doesn't know Dexter well. They aren't neighbors and were never friends. They have known each other since sixth grade, they have shared many classes, but they have never really talked. There's never been any *reason* to talk. Besides, Meredith isn't much of a talker.

With people on Earth, that is.

She has also never been much of a criminal herself and until now she's never sought the company of criminals. It may be a bit much to call Dexter Rigato a criminal (however bad his actions); still, not many mothers would approve of him, and he will certainly never be given a commendation for being Poof Poof Ya.

So Meredith is having a hard time approaching Dexter.

Dexter lingers, too. He doesn't notice Meredith. He's too preoccupied. He sold a fair amount of chatter after those first five words and managed to seem unruffled; nevertheless, he was worried. He still is. He has never been as confident of his power as he might seem. He has always feared that it would get out of hand. That fifth word *may* have been only a solitary glitch, but it worried Dexter.

Finally Meredith blurts, "It's Latin."

Dexter looks at her. "Huh?"

She shrugs and then gets mad at herself for shrugging. More boldly she says, "The fifth word was Latin."

Dexter realizes what she's talking about. He tries to cover himself. "Yeah, I know, so what? I can't use Latin? It sounded cool, so I used it."

"You don't *know* Latin, Dexter. You can't even pass English."

He scowls. "What's your point, Simmons?"

"My point *is,* Rigato, that *I* gave you the word."

He stares at her. "What do you mean?"

"I gave you the *thought.*"

"You're lying."

She pulls a scrap from his notebook. (Dexter's notebook bulges with scraps—most of which are unfinished and overdue homework.) Meredith holds up the scrap and says, "Spray one small word, anything."

"Cost you a quarter."

"I'll give you a dollar."

He is suspicious, of course. But a dollar's a dollar. He shrugs, looks at the paper, and paints *poof.* When he is done, the scrap says: *poof My name is Meredith Simmons and I am inserting these words into Dexter Rigato's brain.*

For probably the first time in his life, Dexter yelps.

Meredith grins and hands him a dollar.

Then she says, "I want a favor."

How many people really know how their blood and muscles work? I know a little, but only because somebody, somewhere, figured it out and put it in a book, and then some teacher told me. If somebody, somewhere, studied my entanglement with Pluto, I am sure they would figure it out and put it in a book, and then I could understand it. At least a little.

But there are lots of things about even normal people that still have never been explained—or if there *is* an explanation, it goes only so far. Everyone just gets used to not knowing things. I'm the same way. I may wonder about it and sure I have my theories, but I don't know how Pluto and I can talk across space, I don't know how his rocks make thoughts, I don't know why God gave Pluto a soul or why it should be joined to mine.

There's more I don't know. I can't explain my connection to Dexter. It makes a certain sense that I would be able to hear his thoughts. He is, so to speak, in *my* house when he paints, and I have spent so many years listening to Pluto's whispers through my roof that Dexter's voice is like a shout beside me. It is more surprising that I could put thoughts into Dexter's head but, after all, that's what I do with Pluto. My thoughts didn't go deep into Dexter's head—they were no more than words, and, in fact, as near as I can tell, they were completely swept out when he painted—but maybe that's only because his head is new to this business and can't handle anything like an entanglement.

Not that I want to be entangled with Dexter Rigato.

For a long time I felt a tingle when I was near Dexter. At first I was afraid that I had some sort of dim-witted crush on him, but when he started his life as Poof Poof Ya, the tingle became a quiet brain hum that clearly had nothing to do with my heart. Then I heard his paint-thoughts and felt them pass to walls and clothes and chatterbooks. I realized that I have no crush *whatsoever* on Dexter Rigato. Thankfully, we are just breathing the same mental air.

After a while I wished that I could do what he does. My power, such as it is, is so private and intimate, and much as that suits me, it can be boring when my only mind-actions are arguments with Pluto. I wished that I could *do* something with my mind, at the very least *contribute* to some physical act. It didn't have to be vandalizing or money making, but it should be something I could actually touch.

Then Pluto wanted to do what I wanted to do.

He knew what I was hoping for when I decided to borrow Poof Poof Ya. I never hid it from him—I've never hidden anything from him. I just hadn't expected him to join in. I hadn't imagined he could. Why should he *want* to? I was hoping to do something using my mind but *outside* of my mind, and Pluto doesn't even quite believe there *is* an outside.

He wanted to participate anyhow. He wanted to *do* something. *Doing* has always amazed him. Only his *Other*-Me had ever done anything; here was a chance for his *Me*-Me to do something. I was wary, though. Then, when I didn't agree right away, he started moping. I finally told him to let me go first— and if everything worked out, then we'd see.

Dexter's mind, apart from the hum, is closed to Meredith— unless he is painting. So she waited for him to paint. She chose a Latin word (from her Missal) so that she would know, when it appeared, that it was definitely hers and not his. Then, when she felt him painting, she threw her word into his spray. She felt her word being tugged. Her word appeared perfectly and harmlessly. This, too, she felt, as her word became written, solid paint. She had not expected such success. She was all awhirl inside.

Because of her excitement she revealed herself to Dexter. She has no reservations about going forward with her wish. There's only a minute or so before class, but *now* is the time. Dexter is off balance and he might agree to her request without a hassle. She wants to get it done before Dexter starts thinking about it too much.

If it goes well, he might let her do it again, some other time.

From a folder she brings out a very nice sheet of firm, ivory paper. It is almost like parchment. She explains to Dexter that she wants to borrow Poof Poof Ya. Dexter frowns. She quickly changes that to *rent*. Dexter stops frowning. Then she asks him to paint the paper *but not to think of anything*. Paint nothing. She will provide all the words.

Meredith is not sure how this will work or if it will. If Dexter does not at least *start* with one of his own words, will there even be anything for her to throw into? Will the spray exist? Besides, can she rely on Dexter to think of nothing and yet paint? He may not have that sort of control.

She does not, however, let him see her doubt. In fact she implies that she could, if she wanted, simply *hijack* Poof Poof Ya, and Dexter could do nothing about it. Dexter is familiar with bluffs like this and he suspects that Meredith is bluffing, but he sees no point in disputing her. As a matter of fact he doesn't want to argue with her at all. He has never cared much for Meredith Simmons (either as an acquaintance or as a girl), but he can't help but be attracted to her, now that he knows she is like him.

To be sure, maybe she is playing a trick on him—maybe she *didn't* use her mind to stick in that Latin word and all—but Dexter doesn't *think* she's tricking him, and even if she is, it's a very good trick and he's impressed.

Without any hassle, Dexter agrees to her request.

Meredith is glad. It isn't much, really, but if she can have a parchment of her very own thoughts, her own little sentimental phrase, she can have some small proof in her hands that there is more to her power than conversing with a distant, grumpy planet.

They agree on a rental fee—Dexter isn't greedy and Meredith doesn't care—and they begin.

To Dexter's surprise, he *is* able to spray nothing. It's no different than pointing a can of spray paint at a wall and spraying random blotches. He lets Meredith guide his hand. She tries to insert her words.

Her words do not appear. *Other* things do—twists, squiggles, scratches, broken shapes—filling the paper like fresh drops of rain on a dry sidewalk, then spilling off and spreading over the table (all terribly *fast*) to Meredith's arms and Dexter's arms and their clothes and faces, and their chairs and their shoes, and the floor, and the kids nearby, and the trays and the plates and the silverware, and the empty milk cartons and the trash, and the walls and the lights and the ceiling, and the lunch ladies, and the exit signs and the halls, and Mr. Chezznik, and the school, and the parking lot, and the trees, the bushes, the cars, the streets, the stores and houses, the lawns and carpets, *all* of it, every surface, every person, every thing. Within seconds, before Dexter can stop it, the entire world is vivid with paint.

Neither Dexter nor Meredith knows, yet, the extent of their disaster, but they can see the cafeteria perfectly well and that is enough to terrify them.

Pluto, on the other hand, is pleased by what he has done.

So now I'm his Furious-Me.

I want to *strangle* him. I imagine my hands around his equator and crushing him to his core. I want to pummel him with comets. I want to shove him into the sun.

I tell Pluto what he's *done*, that he has defaced the entire Earth—even the *clouds* got painted—I yell at Pluto about all the damage he's done and all he can do is cheerfully inform me that his Dark-Me is now his Bright-Me. I *know* it's bright. The only reason *he* knows is that *I* know. He can't see it. I do. I see the bright paint everywhere. But of course I'm his Other-Me. As far as he's concerned, he *does* see it.

Fury is just wasted on Pluto.

It's like lighting matches underwater. He's been so reckless, I've been so careless, my planet has been *ruined,* but none of that matters. He can't understand that any harm has been done. So he was a little impatient. So he went out of turn. So what?

He's happy. He enjoyed his Poof-Poof-Ya-Me. He has now had a taste of *doing.* He didn't know what to make of it, really, since it was so utterly new to him, but he felt it and it *delighted* him. He thinks I should be happy, too. If I weren't in such a bad mood, Pluto's happiness would be the purest in the universe—or (as he puts it) in his Entire-Me. My fury just bemuses him. I try to *explain* and it's like every other time I try to explain. And then what does he do? After I yell and cry and fail to explain and finally wear myself out, he *thanks* me. Poof Poof Ya did Pluto a favor and I was the one who brought them together. Pluto thanks me for that—and then he thanks me for *existing.* He says it can be very good to have an Other-Me. His happiness has reminded him of this. I could think he's simply trying to flatter and disarm me, but I can tell he really means it.

He says it so fondly.

Pluto's word was not any sort of normal word. He couldn't decide on a normal word. Instead he let loose a sound that's been inside him from his beginning, his oldest, most familiar sound, the word that started him. And the weird thing about this word is that it was *inside itself*. It's as if Pluto said *ya* with a *ya* inside, and another *ya* inside that, and another *ya* inside that, on and on, deeper and deeper, forever and ever. Pluto said it only once but it continued saying itself. That's why it spread over the whole world. It even started to cover the Moon. It would have covered all of Creation if Dexter hadn't stopped the spray.

In any event, the Earth is covered.

Fortunately mindpaint isn't toxic, it isn't even paint exactly, it's some kind of adhesive dust. They've been analyzing it. No one knows where it came from or whether it will come again, but they've realized it won't kill anyone. People are still in a kind of panic. The world is clearly covered in some sort of writing. People are afraid of the Writer. Some suppose he could be an angel, but most think he is an alien, and quite a few think he is a demon. While some people analyze the paint itself, others analyze the twists and squiggles. People don't realize, though, that they're trying to translate a brain sneeze.

Meanwhile, there's a scramble for soap and water.

The kids in Meredith's school know where the writing came from. That is, they know it's from Poof Poof Ya. Most of them are really mad at Dexter. Others think he has committed the most awesome act of vandalism ever. He's become a kind of bad-boy god.

Dexter hasn't publicly blamed Meredith. She gives him a lot of credit for that. He refuses to talk to her, though, or even to look at her. He thinks she's dangerous. She's never had a chance to explain what really happened. He wouldn't believe her in any event, since a talking planet is a bit too much to believe.

But the talking planet stays with Meredith.

She is sitting in her bedroom, in her rocking chair. In her hands is the ivory paper. She has removed the paint from her skin and hair—with a lot of soap and scrubbing—but the paper is still covered, like her walls and things and most of the rest of the world. Her parents are working on ways to salvage their household. They've even joined the neighborhood Emergency Clean-up Committee. But it's been only a few days and Pluto's word still fills her room.

She stares at it for a very long time.

She has known all her life that she would never touch Pluto. When she was little she imagined becoming an astronaut and visiting him—but no one is planning to send any ships. Pluto is too far away.

Yet now there is some of him in her room. She even has some of him in her own hand. She stares at the painted ivory paper, at Pluto's word upon it, there to hold.

For a long time, she stares and thinks.

Even when my walls are cleaned and all my stuff is replaced, I want to keep this paper as it is.

I heard this word in my mind, this squiggly, twisting, unending word. I can't read it but I know how it sounds. I know it belongs to Pluto. It's his. It's outside of us but it's with me. Outside of me, but with me.

Like Pluto himself.

I know he still thinks of me as part of himself. I'm sure he always will. Yes, I *am* a girl; I *am* on Earth; Pluto is confused when he thinks otherwise; but even when he does, is he really so terribly wrong? Sometimes I do wonder. I've tried so hard to escape his This-Me and That-Me. Maybe, in the end, he understands our entanglement in the best possible way.

Sure, I say that *now* because he's making me sentimental. He thanks me for being his Other-Me, he fills me with his own happiness, and I get all sentimental. Maybe I *am* disarmed. So I should stop being furious? I don't *think* so. That perfectly happy planet whose soul I share has gone and ruined *my* planet. Someday he has got to admit this. But for now he is fond of me again. It's been a while.

Maybe Poof Poof Ya did me a favor after all.

"THE FIRE SCREAMED UPWARDS, TAKING ME WITH IT."

META HUMAN

Nina has taken me and Henry on lots of adventures, if I can call them that. In the beginning, when Henry and I were first friends, I went along precisely because I was Henry's friend. Yeah, it was a little odd to hang out with my friend and his older sister, but Henry's always been hanging out with Nina. He loves her, after all, and he just wanted to share her with me. I didn't mind at first, since I didn't know Nina that well. And even after I knew Nina well, I still went along. In some ways it's too much bother to resist. Henry doesn't love her any less than he ever did and Henry is still my friend. I like Henry. And probably the only reason he puts up with my attitude about Nina is that he likes me. Besides, he believes in his heart that I'm wrong about her, and he believes, in his heart, that someday I will change my mind.

Nina is sixteen, now.

When she was thirteen, she took us kitty-dropping. We

had a neighbor whose kittens filled his porch. One early morning that summer, with the sun low in a mist and a chill, Nina snatched up a black-and-white kitten and we all scurried back to her garage. In the back, outside, is a tool bin. We had used it before as a step up to the roof. Nina handed the kitten to Henry and climbed up to the roof, and Henry climbed up on the bin and handed her the kitten. Then she told me to make sure the kitten didn't get away. She dropped it. She dropped it upside down. It turned around before it hit and landed on its feet. "Again!" said Nina, and I captured the kitten and gave it to Henry, who gave it to Nina, who gave it to the ground. I can't imagine the kitten was better for it, but it was cool the way it didn't die. Eventually we let it go.

When Nina was fourteen, she took us car-scaring. There's a stretch of road that goes out of our neighborhood and through a field, and alongside it there are ditches. We hid in a ditch. It was cloudy but it hadn't really snowed, and the grass and leaves were dry. Nina had brought a hammer. She was going to throw the hammer at a passing car. Well, not *actually* throw it. "If you *throw* it," she said, "you can only do this once." A car sped towards us and Nina popped up out of the ditch, waved the hammer so the driver saw it, and swung. The car swerved as it went past. Nina huddled down again, laughing. We heard the next car. Henry took the hammer and swung it. This car swerved, too, but kept going. The third car, the one I scared, slammed to a stop on the shoulder. The driver roared out of his car and came at us. We ran.

We got away. On the way home, along a fence, we found some empty bottles and broke them with the hammer.

When Nina was fifteen, she took us pipe-walking. Many blocks away there's this factory, and inside the grounds there are these huge circular pits, filled with sewage or some sort of waste, speckled, thick, and awful smelling. A snarl of pipes goes into the center of each pit, six feet above the waste until they bend straight down. We got onto the factory grounds through a gap in the fence. No one stopped us at the pits. It's not like they're guarded. Nina said, "I'll go first," and she climbed onto a pipe and walked out to the center of a pit, and there, above the waste and under a nasty sun, with all the insects making a racket, Nina put her feet together and hopped ten times. We had no idea how deep the pits were. She came back and said it was Henry's turn, but he wouldn't go and neither would I. We might risk the lives of kittens and drivers, but we weren't ready to risk our own. So Nina went in our places, hopping ten times for Henry and ten for me.

Sure, she might have fallen and died.

It didn't make any difference to her.

So let me tell you something, flat out: Nina's messed up. If Henry heard me say that, he'd probably slug me. But I'm sorry—that's just how it is. Nina is reckless. She can get kind of nasty, too. And she gets that way often. Even now she does. So don't expect her to get nice by the end of it all. She never had a change of heart. If Nina's heart had changed, Paul might be alive.

See, Paul died.

Nina could have saved him.

She wouldn't.

I

Nina is a metakid, which means she has a power.

Her power is odd.

She can fly if she wants, but first she has to give herself the power to fly. She has to say to herself: "Now I can fly." She can say it in her head, although she tends to declare it out loud; either way, if she says she can fly, she can fly. But at that point, flying is *all* she can do (apart from her normal human stuff). If later she decides she wants to see through walls, she has to say, "Now I can see through walls," and sure enough she can—but then she can't fly anymore. She can do only one metathing at a time.

But she can do any metathing she wants.

No one gave Nina this power. She didn't meet some magical little man in some magical little shop, who sold her some magical little potion. Her power just appeared out of nowhere, from no one, about a month ago. No one has come to ask for a thank-you or a payment.

And Nina's not the only one with a power.

Henry has his own power, too. Nina gave it to him. It was a gift. Nina's messed up, sure, but she's not inhuman. She knows Henry loves her and I think she really loves him back. That's only human, right? And it's a strange gift, I suppose, but out of love she made Henry a metakid.

It was simple, really. Nina said, "Now I can give a power to Henry." She couldn't make him like herself. She tried but she can't. Henry can't change his own power but he can have whatever single power Nina gives him. She finally gave him the power to change elements. He can turn a tin can into a gold can, and stuff like that. There's no special reason that she picked this power. It was simply the thirty-seventh one that they tried out before Nina got tired of all the fuss and said, "That's it, Henry, *this* is your power."

Henry didn't mind. Whatever the power, he was thrilled. He's always wanted to be a metahuman. He's *really* into comic books. Every other day he'd show me some comic book and, pointing at some metahuman in it, say: "I could be that guy, *easy*, if I wasn't so normal."

Then Nina gave powers to me and Louise.

Henry asked her to do it. It amused her to do it. She did it without our permission, although that wasn't Henry's idea; but he was glad anyway that she did it. He wanted us both to be metakids, too. I'm his friend, after all—and so is Louise. Yeah, Louise may be *my* girlfriend, but Henry likes her as well—not the way *I* do, but just the way he likes people.

Henry is full of like.

In any event, the day that it happened, Louise and I were sitting on her porch, talking together, covered by sunlight and the shadows of leaves, when Henry and Nina came over. Henry had visited Louise before, with me that is, but Nina never had. She hadn't come to visit now. She had come to be dramatic. She told Henry, who was giddy, to hush, and she crossed her arms, glared at us, and told us, smugly: "You two aren't human anymore." Of course she had to explain what she meant—she explained about her power and what she had done to us—and of course we didn't believe her. To prove the point about being meta, Henry gladly turned some leaves into aluminum; and Nina said, "Now I can be a mist," and she swirled around us mistily. Louise yelped. So did I. "You see?" said Nina, her mist fluttering in our ears. "That's what you are. Like me and Henry. I gave *you* the fire, Jake. That's your power. You can make fire out of nothing—and control it." She thickened around Louise. "And little Miss Cavanaugh here can shrink or grow. Go ahead, *dear*. Stop being short."

That stung Louise, a little, and I told Nina she didn't have to be nasty. Nina didn't answer. She simply waited. Suddenly Louise stood up. The Nina-mist blew aside. Louise wasn't really angry at Nina's insult. And she hadn't stood up out of fear, although she was afraid. It was more that she was ready to stand *against* whatever was going on. If she had to. But she wasn't sure yet. And she told me later that she was as curious as anyone would be. So, cautiously, she became a foot taller. Louise stared at herself, simply fascinated. Henry cheered. Louise shrank back to normal. She sat down, close to me, and became very quiet.

Still cheerful, Henry told me to make a fire. Timidly I lit the end of my finger. It didn't hurt. But it was a flame. I stopped it, it vanished. Not knowing what else to say, I said: "Wow."

"So there you are," said Nina.

I wondered if any neighbors had been watching. I didn't

see any. Nina didn't seem to care. She was still a mist. I could have told myself it wasn't real, but everything was so *obviously* real. Except for the metastuff, it was just an afternoon on Louise's porch—and it stayed that way, second after second, sunlight, shadows, breeze on my neck, someone's radio playing in someone's house. I know what real is like. That flame I made was real.

I told Nina she could have *asked* us first. She said, "What, you don't like it?" Oh, I liked it all right. As a matter of fact, the first time I made a white-hot fireball hover in my hand, I *loved* it. But to become a metakid, out of the blue, was just too weird. At least a warning would have been nice. Nina thought I was being ungrateful. She became her normal self again and said, "Quit your griping. You want me to take it back?"

"No!" I cried. Already I knew I would miss it.

"Then shut up and keep it." She stared at Louise. "Your girlfriend, too. Maybe someday you'll have a bunch of superbabies." She said to Henry, "I'll see *you* later. Now I can pop out of here." She sent herself away.

She was gone.

Henry wanted to stay and maybe all of us practice with our powers, but Louise said she didn't want to, not then, and he figured she wanted to get back to her time alone with me, so he said, "Sure, okay," and happily walked back to his own house.

I asked Louise if she was okay. She shrugged. "I don't know."

"I'm sorry about what Nina said. She's not too polite."

"That's okay."

"Does it bug you that she didn't ask us?"

"Yes, a little. No, a lot. But that's not it." She closed her hand and opened it. "It's just so *unnatural*, Jake. I don't know what to *think*."

"So don't think," I said. "Just say it's great."

She looked at me. "Is it?"

"Isn't it?"

She sighed. "I don't know."

Louise has been my girlfriend for only a while. In fact I'm still trying to figure this out. The whole thing with her is kind of unexpected. At least *I* never expected it. I mean, there's all these girls I'd see at school, and I'd wonder which one of them might like me and I'd try not to act too stupid, just so they *might* like me, but I have to admit that I really didn't try that hard; and even if I wasn't *that* stupid (who knows what the girls think of me), not much ever came of anything and I stopped expecting things to happen, at least for a while.

Then there was Louise.

She doesn't go to my school. She goes to Our Lady Queen of Martyrs. But she lives across the street from Henry and for a couple of years I had seen her around. She keeps to herself but she doesn't keep to her house. If she's not sitting on her porch reading a book or watching the sky, she's taking a quiet walk. She's always been visible enough and, yeah, I saw her, but until recently I didn't really care.

One day, a month ago, I was on my way to Henry's. This was before Nina had gone meta. Louise was out on one of her walks. We were on the same side of the street. She was coming towards me. I was ready to nod to her, out of politeness, I guess, or just because I couldn't ignore her like some sort of clod, when she said, just as she passed me, "Hi, Jake," and she passed me, and I turned to say something, too, but I had never really said, "Hi, Louise," before, or anything at all to her, so I hesitated, and it was all a lot weirder than it should have been—especially when I noticed she was walking faster, as if she was suddenly embarrassed.

For some reason, I liked my name in her voice.

That just got me wondering and then I noticed her a lot more, and the *next* time we passed I said, "Hi, Louise," and she said hi to me, and soon we would say a little more—just talking—and at first it was talking just to talk, since we didn't have much to share at first. Even though we had been in the same neighborhood for years and had picked up each other's names, we didn't know all that much about each other.

I knew one big thing about Louise. You hear things about the people in your neighborhood. I had heard that Louise Cavanaugh tries to be good. And it's true. Yeah, there are stuck-up kids who try to be good because they think they're better than you, but I learned that Louise isn't like that.

You know what she *is* like?

There's this girl in our neighborhood—Margo Tyler—who was telling lies about Louise, nothing extreme but nothing nice, either, and people were believing her. Louise and I were talking one day, out on the street, when Margo and her friends came near. They were laughing about one of the lies.

Louise heard. I heard. Louise didn't deny it or try to fight, she only ran away. I didn't know what to do. I gave Margo a dirty look but my looks don't matter to her. I wanted to hit her or something. She's such a witch. She went away, laughing, with her friends. I ran after Louise. She had stopped on the other side of a tree. Her eyes were closed. She wasn't crying. She wasn't even upset, not exactly. Her hands were together. She was praying. I figured she was praying for help from God, like asking God to vaporize Margo or at least make her nice or something. I waited for Louise to finish. I always wait when Louise prays. Soon she crossed herself and opened her eyes. She said, "Oh. Hi, Jake." I asked her if she thought God would really stop Margo. Louise said she hadn't prayed for that. She had asked God not to hate Margo. I told her she *should* have asked God to put a nuclear blast in Margo's gut. Louise shook her head the way she does—in this kind of tremble—and she told me, "Oh, no, Jake, you're supposed to pray *for* your enemies, not against them."

That's what Louise is like.

That's not much what I'm like, though. I never really have been. If I'm good, it's only because I'm not being bad. Hey, I'm not a delinquent. I've got nothing against the rules. I'm just lazy. Being good is just too much work—especially when it comes to praying for your enemies.

And that's what confuses me about this thing with Louise and me. Oh, I really like her now and I'm pretty sure she likes me, but we're not exactly a match. I don't know what caught her eye in the first place. She didn't say hi to me, that first time, just to say hi. She was trying to *start* something. She started something, all right—but why *me*? What caught her eye? I don't know. But whatever it was, it hasn't let go of her yet.

Soon after we got our powers, Nina took us prison-wrecking.

They say it's a prison. It was probably just a special boarding school. There aren't any walls or fences, except for the trees, and it doesn't look like there ever were. But they say the kids who lived here were insane. I don't know. The only sign at the gate says:

NO TRESPASSING

GOVERNMENT PROPERTY

The government doesn't try very hard to keep anyone out. The gate can keep out cars, but that's all. It's low enough to jump over and you don't even *have* to jump. You can walk around it easy.

Then there's a road. Next to the road, near the gate, is a soccer field. There's a perfect row of old trees. Between the trees are bits of forest. The soccer field is just a field, now.

Next to the field is a gray swing set with no swings.

Along the road there's all sorts of buildings—a firehouse, a theater, a bunch of dorms—and they all have the same look. The tiles on every roof are clay, like pottery, and cracked and tossed to the ground. The windows are smashed and twisted and dangling and jagged. The walls are brick and aren't so very damaged, not like you'd think, apart from the random soot and crumbling and of course the curls of obnoxious painted words and pictures; but the buildings are so *empty* that the walls seem fake or pointless or something. You go inside through some hole—or through some doorway without a door—and you might see a cupboard kicked on the floor or a desk knocked into a corner or a couple of cabinets on their sides like they lost a fight and just don't care anymore, but mostly it's just pebbles of glass, flakes of paint, and other things to crunch under your feet.

None of this has happened on its own. The prison may be abandoned but it's not ignored. Lots of kids get in there. You go to destroy. Break a window and no one cares. Throw a toilet at a wall and no one knows. Start a fire and you'll only be burning someone else's ashes. Some workers do come, you know, now and then, and they're slowly demolishing the prison. But it's only their job. For most of the kids who come here, demolition is a joy. And they can't be kept away. Some of the buildings have tape across their openings and signs that say:

DANGER

ASBESTOS

CANCER AND LUNG HAZARD

AUTHORIZED PERSONNEL ONLY

RESPIRATORS AND PROTECTIVE CLOTHING

ARE REQUIRED IN THIS AREA

I guess there's asbestos in the walls or something and the workers are removing it. The workers tear asbestos from the walls and fill the air with asbestos dust, and then put up their signs and tape and go home; and then the kids show up in their T-shirts and sneakers and tear down the signs and tape and go into the buildings and breathe asbestos and break things.

If the prison *wasn't* for insane kids, it is now.

Sometimes I've gone to the prison on my own. It's easy to go, so I go. I tell myself I'm not as bad as the other kids. I don't start fires, I don't spray-paint the walls, I don't find some corner to smoke or drink; but I do break a thing, now and then, and of course whenever I'm there I'm completely trespassing. I'm where I shouldn't be.

But what the heck.

Louise had never been to the prison on her own. She's not the kind to trespass, let alone demolish, and if a sign tells her to keep out, she keeps out. I had never taken her there, either. I wouldn't want to. The place is so dead it can't even be haunted. It's worn down and misused and there's nothing there for Louise. She wouldn't have gone anyhow.

But Nina wanted us all to go, even Louise. Up until then Henry and I had been using our powers carefully, calmly, even timidly, in the basement or the garage; and Louise had done even less. Nina didn't want us timid in our houses anymore. She wanted us to *USE* our powers—to "stop being pansies," she said—and she picked the prison because it's the place to pick, really, when you want to be abnormal. Besides, there wouldn't be any gawkers. You can get some serious solitude in the prison. It's a big place and the kids aren't always swarming over it.

I agreed to go. The prison was familiar to me and I figured that if we got clumsy we couldn't do any damage that mattered. Henry also agreed to go, but that was no surprise. Henry wants whatever Nina wants. And in any event, he and I are used to these sorts of things. It was just another of Nina's adventures.

Only Louise hesitated. She didn't want to disobey the signs. She wondered if we'd be caught. She was afraid that even if we weren't caught, she would have to lie to her parents about where she had been. I told her we would make sure she didn't have to lie. She asked me how we would do that. I had no idea. I thought she was worrying too much, but I don't like to see her worry. I was about to suggest some other place when Nina sighed angrily and impatiently and, looking upwards, cried, "*Geez*, Louise, tell them the truth. Say, 'Momma and Dadda, I went to the Prison School for Utterly Insane Children and me and my superpowered friends made a mess of the place.'"

Nina's anger and impatience got Louise to come. Maybe Louise would have resisted more if I had resisted more. She told me later that while we were in the prison, she just pretended she was at the park. Her parents never asked her where she had been, and that night she made an act of contrition and apologized to God.

None of us talked to each other on the way to the prison. We didn't have a chance. Nina took Henry's hand, Henry took Louise's, Louise took mine, and Nina said: "Now I can run like a laser." I'm not so sure Nina was really running—not with her feet, anyhow. We went so fast that everything was distorted. We didn't hit any of it. We went through it all. We were a blast of ghosts.

Somehow Nina knew when to stop. And we stopped. I wasn't dizzy. I hadn't been turned inside out. I didn't feel a burn from speed or a bruise from passing though the world. Not even my mother would have found a thing wrong with me. But why should she have? It was such a tiny thing, after all, just a yank through hyperspace. Nothing abnormal in *that*.

Nina let go of Henry. Henry let go of Louise. Louise took a step closer to me and tightened her hand on mine. I suppose that made her feel safer, and sure I like it when she holds my hand, but if Nina had felt like yanking us again through hyperspace I doubted that I could have stopped her, not even to protect Louise. Maybe there was really no need to protect her. But I squeezed Louise's hand to let her know I would have tried.

We had ended up in the prison theater. I had been there before. I had been into most of the places in the prison, except for the underground tunnels. I wouldn't go into the tunnels. Call me yellow if you want, but there was no way I would ever lower myself into *those* places. But the theater I'd go into. It was easy to escape from the theater if you had to.

There were no seats. There was only a plain of rubble. Along the front of the stage there used to be lights; now there were only sockets, pulled out of the stage but connected by wires and twisting down to the floor like some train off a cliff.

Over the stage, hanging from rods high in the ceiling, were all sorts of cables. I suppose that once upon a time the cables were used to raise boats on cardboard waves or lower angels on plastic wings.

Nina jumped up on the stage. "It's all ours!" she cried, spreading her arms. Then she stared at us so hard. She raised her finger like she was scolding us and said, "Don't you *dare* do anything useful."

She turned from us and said something I couldn't hear. She must have been calling up a new power, because she started growing blades. They pushed out of her. Her clothes were ripped but she didn't seem to mind. Every blade was very bright, like water in the sun. Some were wide as machetes; some were thin as needles. Nina swung her arm at a cable and the cable sprinkled to the ground, sliced in a hundred places. She cried "Ha!" and started walking around the stage, among the cables, along the walls, slicing as she went. She took her time, almost dreamily, leaving razor wounds even in the brick.

Louise asked, "Why is she *doing* that?"

I told her, "That's just how Nina is."

Henry glared at me and I was sorry I said it. Louise didn't know Nina as well as I did, because she hadn't known Henry as long as I had. Henry is perfectly aware of my opinions about Nina. We more or less agreed, a long time ago, that I have no right to judge her. I had gotten so used to *not* judging her I had sort of forgotten she is the kind of person who almost *asks* to be judged. Oh, sure, you could say that Nina was doing nothing more than what *I* did at the prison. Both of us went there to add to the damage. Even so, it was the *way* she was doing it. Yeah, fine, I broke things, but she was *killing* them. Not in anger, no. It was like she was walking through a garden and cheerfully beheading flowers.

In fact it was just a little more weird than usual. It was kind of *ugly*. Watching Nina scatter gashes around the stage, I started to regret letting Louise into this. It was all well and good to be metakids, but I wasn't so sure I wanted our powers to be a gift from *Nina*.

I had my power, though, and Louise had hers, and I didn't want to make her all fretful over Nina. I didn't want to be fretful myself. So I backed away from my thoughts, ignored the blades, let Henry go off by himself (because I had insulted his sister), and then took Louise to the balcony, where we could be a pair of metakids all alone and without a worry in the world.

The graffiti was pretty dense in the theater and the balcony was quite colorful, not like a rainbow but in a pukish sort of way. Some of it was as worn away as the plaster. There were the usual bad words and names of rock stars, and a few of those happy faces with *X*s for eyes. The *X*-eyed happy faces were all over the prison, along with the initials G.y.F. I don't know what "G.y.F." means. In front of Louise and me, on the bottom riser, was the outline of a kid who had sprawled on the ground. It looked like the outline of a murdered gingerbread man.

Louise asked me if I was going to use my power and I told her probably, but I wasn't in a hurry, and I didn't mind just sitting with her. She smiled at that. I wasn't trying to get a smile but I take them when I get them—and with Louise at least, it's easy to give them back. Then we both watched Henry and Nina down below.

Henry was out in the open space where the seats were gone. He was squatting like he was watching tadpoles in a pond. He reached down and touched a board and most of the wood became some purple crystal. Then he touched a few stones, one after the other, and they each became a puff of green gas and orange dust.

Nina scooted up behind him. She was done with the hanging cables and the stage. Her blades were gone. She looked normal, apart from the thousands of rips in her clothes. Henry didn't notice her at first. She got in front of him with a single wide step. He was a little startled but all he did was say, "Hey, Nina."

"Go ahead, Worm Boy. Touch my foot."

If Nina had asked *me* to touch her foot, like that, out of the blue, I would have said, "What the heck *for*?" You would have said it, too. Henry didn't. And usually if someone calls *me* a worm, I get a fist ready. But Nina didn't mean anything cruel by what she said. Nina is never cruel to Henry. She called him "Worm Boy" because she has called him "Worm Boy" ever since he was five. When Henry was five he had surgery. The scar ran down his chest. It swelled up a bit. It looked like a worm.

Henry still has the worm on his chest. It's nothing much, now, and he doesn't really feel it, but for a while the scar was so deep, so painful, the stitches so tight, that he couldn't even sit up straight; and even after the stitches were gone, the swelling stayed and was sore for the longest time. However much it hurt him, though, the worm delighted Nina. It was proof that Henry hadn't died when he might have. Besides, it was funny. It was not supposed to be there.

So anyhow, because Nina told him to, Henry touched her foot.

And she shuddered and grabbed at her face and screamed. All of her, her body, her clothes, her hair, became metallic. She melted into a shape of herself, flowing bright and like a mirror; and the shadows of all her details, in her eyes, her ears, the bends of her fingers, mixed with the reflections of everything around her. She had not become a statue. She folded at her knees and put out her hands to Henry. She never quite lost her shape but it seemed to move ahead of itself. Her scream broke into sputtering sobs and she cried, "How *could* you!"

Henry was laughing. "How could I *what*?"

She spread her arms. "*You*, Mr. Alchemist, Mr. Element Changer! You turned your own sister into *mercury*!"

Henry stopped laughing. He even pulled back. "Nina, are you *really* mercury?"

"Calm down, Worm Boy." She was smiling. "*You* didn't really do it. I gave myself the power—"

"No, I mean are you really *mercury*?"

She shrugged. "I said I was."

"But mercury's poisonous!"

"Yeah, no kidding. But it's so *gorgeous*."

Henry all but lunged at Nina and flicked his hand at her

knee. The mercury became dull and dark. Nina stiffened. She forced her head to turn and she looked at herself. "Henry," she groaned, "you turned me . . . into . . . what did you—?"

"Iron."

"*Iron.*"

"Sorry! It's all I could think of."

"Yes, well. Now I can be mercury again." And she was. She drew her hand in front of her face, watching her fingers reflect her eyes. "You know, Henry, just 'cause it's poisonous—Man! That was an awfully *useful* thing to do." She stood up. "Now I can disappear."

And she did.

Henry looked back and forth, waiting for her to reappear. She didn't. Then he looked at his hand—the hand that had touched her—looking for specks of mercury, I am sure; but I guess it had all been changed.

He waited for Nina a while longer.

Then he went back to his alchemy.

Nina reappeared beside Louise.

Nina's little horror show, with the screaming and all, had upset Louise at first. Even though she realized that Nina was faking, she was still a bit shaken; and so when Nina appeared, like a snap, right beside her, Louise let out a good-sized, almost terrified yelp.

Nina snickered. Then she said, "Hm. Never mind. Now I can be any girl. No—*every* girl."

She started flickering through identities. Every instant she was a different girl. I recognized every sort of dress I'd ever seen in a social studies book, and every sort of face. She stepped around Louise and over to me, and, from the back, put her hands on my shoulders, and the skin of her hands wouldn't stop changing, white, black, and everything in between. When she spoke, she spoke with voices from everywhere, all in English, yeah, but not from *our* neighborhood. Her words were spoken by a million strangers.

She said, "You seem spooked, Jake. You don't like me this way?"

I shrugged under her hands. "Maybe not."

"But you have to like me sooner or later. I'm every girl there is." She leaned closer to my ear. "Hey, I might even be *Louise,* sooner or later. It's a small world after all, Jake. Sooner or later I'll be a mousy little American teenager. Right, Louise?"

"Hey!" I cried.

Louise didn't know what to say. I think she was repulsed.

"Poor Louise. Poor Jake. Be that as it may." She tightened her hands. "So, Jakey. What gives? I give you guys the bestest toys ever and you sit up here on your butts."

"We'll get around to it, Nina."

"Will you, now? But you can call up *fire.* Why wait? Haven't you ever wanted to *burn*?"

"Huh?"

"*Burn*! Haven't you ever wanted to go into a crowd, out in a mall, or in a plaza, yeah, in the middle of the afternoon, and *ignite*?"

I cringed.

"No, *no*," she said, "I don't mean to hurt anyone—just to *startle* them. To become a *column of flame,* where once you were yourself."

"I dunno—"

"C'mon, Jake! To raise a *holocaust* to the sky—and make the people wonder *how* it could be that little old *you,* little old boring, *boring* Jake is the source—the *soul!*—of the fire that *stands* before them, as tall as the heavens. *You,* the fire that toasts their ties and blackens their skirts and singes their beautiful hair. Eh, Jake?"

I didn't exactly give her an answer, so she kept jabbing me, saying this, saying that, even digging her nails into me once. Finally I'd had it. I stood up, almost knocking her backwards, and raised my arm and fist. If she wanted fire, I'd give her fire. As I chose a target, I realized that I was kind of posing, like all I needed was a costume and a word balloon above my head; but I didn't care. There's a reason for those poses. They say: *Watch out, here it comes, something more than human.*

I saw a poster on the wall. It was part of the original decoration, more like a wallpaper painting. Patches of missing plaster had taken away most of it; enough remained, although even that was peeling away. It had been a picture of an oasis. You could just make out some men and their camels. The palm trees were very tall.

I opened my fist and felt the fire swirl around my hand. My fire doesn't burn me. I don't even feel its heat. It gathers on my skin and waits to go.

I let it go.

The oasis went away.

But that was all. The paper died but the plaster killed the fire. Just as well, I suppose, since I didn't want to torch the theater, but it *was* a sissy effect: *whoof, crackle, sizzle, puff,* done. I had wasted my pose on a dud.

Nina sighed. "Pure apocalypse, Jake. Got me shakin'." She turned to Louise. "Think you can do better, dear? Become a Titan for us."

Louise shook her head, not in her usual tremble but very slowly, very emphatically no.

"*Geez,* Louise. What a couple of lame-oids."

Nina left us. She didn't disappear, she didn't leap in a single bound, she didn't sprint through the eighty-third dimension. She just got up and walked away. She was still in her girl flicker. It gave me a headache.

I looked away.

Louise seemed grim. Nina had not been kind to her. Louise is not so thin skinned, however. It takes a lot to put her down.

I asked her what was wrong.

She said, "Wrong? You want a *list?*"

"No. I can guess."

She paused. She asked me, carefully, as though *I* might get offended, "Has Nina *always* been like this?"

I said, "Yeah."

And Louise shook her head, sadly.

Henry thinks I'm too harsh about Nina. Maybe sometimes I am. I didn't even hesitate when I answered Louise. Of *course*

Nina's always been like this. And then I remembered something Nina had done. I could have told Louise about Nina's prayer for Henry.

It was Henry, of course, who told me about the prayer. Nina has told me lots of things about herself, whether I wanted to know them or not, but she never told me this.

Henry was born with a hole in his heart. Not on the outside, but inside, between the part where the blood goes in and the part where it goes out. Calling it a "hole" is enough, but the medical term is "ventricular septal defect"—and the only reason I mention *that* is because that's what Henry calls it: his Ventricular Septal Defect, almost like he's describing a nifty malfunction in a robot or something. It's fixed now, of course—I mean, that was the whole point of his surgery—but until he was five, half his blood that should have left his heart sloshed back through the hole. He wasn't getting the oxygen he should have and he got tired very easily.

But they had to let him grow up that way, because until he was five he wasn't strong enough to have his heart cut open and sewn.

Henry remembers most of his time in the hospital. It's hard not to. He remembers afterwards, being in his bed, stitches in his chest, tubes and wires connecting him to machines like roots to the dirt. He remembers right before the surgery, when the anesthesiologist talked to him about cars. He remembers waiting to be taken to the operating room and his mother reading him a comic book to keep him calm. They came to take him and he wouldn't let her stop reading. She followed alongside the bed, down the hallway to the operating room, hunching over so that he could see the pictures. At the doors she had to leave him. He had never really understood what was happening. His mother had been afraid to tell him everything. He turned to look back at her and called, "Mommy, what are they going to do to me?"

He doesn't remember his mother crying then, because she was out of sight, but he found out later. And he found out later, much later, that Nina, who was waiting at home, was sure that Henry was going to die. At that time Nina was only seven, but she was on her way to being what she is now. She had already decided that Santa Claus is stupid. She had decided the same thing about God. Mostly she just hated going to church. But because Henry might die, Nina got scared, and she asked God not to take him away. She wasn't so sure that God would listen. She hadn't been very nice to him lately. So to make her prayer stronger, she went into Henry's room and gathered up some of his toys and lined them up, across and down, in the shape of a crucifix, and said her prayer again.

I suppose God was pleased. Henry's still here, in any event.

Louise would have seen hope in this. Even though it was nine years ago—more than half of Nina's life ago—Louise would have called it proof that there's a drop of goodness in Nina, somewhere; something that can't grow blades and doesn't long to burn itself in a public place.

Maybe. If the drop hasn't dried up.

In a way, this "drop of goodness" was Henry's thinking, too, when he told me about it. He was defending Nina from my bad attitude about her. How awful could a person be, after all, who makes such a prayer?

But I didn't want to bring all this up, not then, not there in the prison. It was kind of secret, for one thing. I wasn't so sure that Henry would want Louise to know. Besides, for all I knew, Nina had made herself invisible and was sitting right in front of Louise and me, spying on what we said about her. It was easier just to say that Nina had never been any different, no matter what she had done when she was seven years old and scared.

II

I had gone to the prison more or less thinking that we could practice in a big and messy way. Nina took us there just to keep us from minding our lives. Whatever our reasons, it was a wasted trip. After talking to Louise and me, Nina called the whole thing off. I think we had annoyed her. Then again, Nina often ends what she starts before it has finished.

Anyhow, she returned to Henry, looked up at us, and yelled, "Now I can send you all home." And I found myself at home. Not even a push through hyperspace, not that I saw. I was just suddenly someplace else. Louise wasn't with me. I ran to the phone to call her house and she answered on the first ring. She had been about to call me. Then I called Henry and he, too, was home, and he was a little mad. He wanted to know what we had said to Nina. I sort of told him what had happened, but not like it was our fault. He grumbled and said he'd talk to me later. Then he hung up.

The next day, on my way to Henry's, I stopped by Louise's. While I was talking to her I mentioned that Henry and I were going to practice some more. She asked to join us. That surprised me. I hadn't thought that she would *want* to practice with us, especially after the thing in the prison. I asked her, "Are you sure?"

"Yeah. I think so."

"Really?"

"I think so. Probably. You think I shouldn't?"

"It's not that. I mean . . . you weren't too happy yesterday."

"You're right, I wasn't. But that was because of Nina, and the way she was acting, and because of where we were."

"It had nothing to do with our powers?"

"Um. Not really." She squinted at me the way she sometimes does. "I don't think my *power* is bad. I can shrink. I can grow. Is that bad? True, I have to wonder where it came from. I wonder about Nina. Because we're mixed up with *her*, I went to that prison. *I broke a law*. Every second we were there I told myself, 'Pretend you're at the park,' and for half a second I *could* pretend—but I knew what I was really doing, and you know what? I kept doing it. It was *my* fault. I can't blame Nina. I can't blame my power. The power may be a temptation, the situation may not be good, and I know there are some situations you *know* are bad and you can recognize them and stay away, but whatever I *do* will be *my* fault. Besides, I'm not so sure about this situation. For all I know, God might be testing me. I don't want to run away from his tests. I want to *pass* them. I know I mustn't do bad things, not even by mistake, but I can sin only if I choose to sin—and I won't choose to sin anymore."

Louise has this way of making even small things *real* intense. There I was, afraid she might have been slightly put out by all of this, and she's winding her way through fault and sin. Before then I had regretted the *ugliness* of this nonsense with Nina, not the *danger*. I was worrying that Louise might get mud on her dress and all the while she's worrying about the stains on her soul. I don't know if I'll ever understand why everything with her always comes down to that.

Talking to Louise made me realize something.

Until I had my power, I had never started a fire in the prison. I had told myself that only the truly bad kids, only the *real* punks, started fires. Okay, sure, you could say that I *had* started mine in a kind of temper tantrum and it hadn't amounted to much in any event. You could say that. Then again, a fire's a fire and maybe I *was* a punk after all—yeah, not much of a punk, but even so—or else starting fires isn't something that makes you a punk.

See what talking to Louise can do to you?

Well, I didn't fret over it. It was done and *done* and we weren't in the prison anymore. I suppose I could have made an act of contrition, just like Louise, but I didn't know the words exactly and, besides, I wasn't so sure what I'd be apologizing for. It's not like I *murdered* somebody or something. Like God really cares about all the stupid things I do!

He's got to have more on his mind than me.

So the three of us got together and practiced.

It was only us three. Nina wasn't around. Henry didn't know where she had gone, but she had left the house by folding herself out of sight. I made some crack about it being just as well. I didn't mean anything *harsh*, it was just a crack; but it made Henry scowl. I really should shut up more often. It isn't fair to Henry. Sometimes he must feel stuck between me and Nina.

The three of us weren't practicing for anything special. It's not like we were training for the Meta Olympics. In fact, "practice" is probably too big a word. We were just seeing what we could do. It was summer, that's all. And without Nina around, it never got ugly. We were just goofing off. Having fun. Playing a game.

Nothing else to do.

We went to the woods. The woods are nearby, still full of tall trees, just an unfinished chunk of our neighborhood. We went in, and down, towards the creek. It's not much of a creek. It's more like a running puddle. We chose the woods because, like the prison, there are spots where you can't be seen. We were tired of basements and garages but we still didn't want any gawkers. After all, if nothing else, the freakishness of it all could be embarrassing.

Henry also wanted us to keep our *secret identities*. No one could know that Henry, Jake, and Louise were more than human. In fact, Henry took it a step further than that: As humans, yes, we were "Henry," "Jake," and "Louise"; as *meta*humans, though, we needed *meta*names.

Or so Henry figured.

Of course, Henry already had a metaname. He was already Worm Boy. Okay, this Worm Boy business might seem a *little* odd, but over the years Henry has taken it as a kind of destiny. "Worm Boy" has the sound, of course, of a superhero's name, and Nina has always filled it with such affection that it never seemed to Henry that a worm was not a thing for a hero to be. What counts, for Henry, is being one of the metahumans, and there are already so many named for spiders, beetles, wolverines, and hawks, that there has to be a place for a worm.

Alchemy, however, isn't very wormy. Henry might never stop being a Worm Boy, but he had started being something else besides and for *that,* he needed an appropriate name. Just as Louise and I needed appropriate names. So on the way to the woods, Henry got us talking about it. I can't say that Louise and I really cared one way or the other, but Henry certainly cared. He went through all sorts of names, from good ones like "Blaze" (for me) to lame ones like "Sizes Girl" (for Louise). Although nothing, in the end, appealed to us, and nothing really came of our conversation, it was a way to kill time as we walked.

After a while we found a good spot.

We had no particular plan. Henry gladly started us off. He

was getting good at using his power. He had been reading about the chemical makeup of things, so he could know what he needed for this thing or that, and by mixing and matching his elements he could make sugar from stones and acids from air. Sure, maybe the sugar wasn't *really* sugar—I wouldn't taste it, none of us would, so we have no idea if Henry got it right—but the acid certainly hissed when it hit the ground. And the ammonia he made from a pair of twigs, the nitroglycerin from an old cocoon, the strings of copper from a spider's web: All of it stank or banged or glittered in just the way you would have expected.

Then Louise said she had an idea. She wouldn't tell us, though. She seemed a little embarrassed. But then she took a branch and dug a tiny trench, five feet long, down towards the creek but not reaching it, and in the top of this trench she put a pile of pebbles and leaves. She pointed at the pile and said to Henry, "Um, make it gold," and he did, and she told me, "Now melt it, slowly," and I did—with a steady fire—and it flowed through the trench she had made. Then she looked at us and bit her lip and smiled nervously, then instantly shrank herself to the size of a fairy and sat on a stone beside the gold.

I asked her, "What *are* you doing?"

She grinned. "Sitting beside my river of gold."

Louise can get fanciful, sometimes.

The heat was too much for her, though—at *her* size, that is—so after a few moments she grew big again. I had stopped my fire and the gold now cooled, and Henry and I waited for Louise to do something else.

But when she noticed us watching her, she said, "Why are you staring? What, was that a weird thing to do?"

I shook my head. "No, that's not it, I was just waiting for you to do something else."

"So am I," said Henry.

"Oh," she said.

Louise, though, was still cautious about using her power. For a minute or so she had been a fairy, but that didn't mean she was ready to continue with things. She had sipped from her power but had no plans to gulp.

"C'mon," I said.

"Yeah," said Henry.

"Well." She paused. "All right."

She looked around, to make sure we really were unseen, and checked the branches above her, and carefully became a giant. Not *gigantic*, but just way bigger than a person should be. She started to sink into the dirt from her added weight and Henry told her to lift her left foot, and then her right, and he made the ground beneath them into concrete, to hold her up. She lost her balance and slipped on her ankle, twisting it slightly, but she grabbed at a tree trunk and didn't fall. I watched Louise grow and I kept expecting it to look like a bad special effect, but of course it was perfect, because it was perfectly real.

I think she felt too *obvious*, though, being over twenty feet tall, and after only a few seconds she shrank back down. As soon as she was normal again she said it was my turn, and we said no, she should do some more, but she said,

"Maybe later," and she told me to go ahead. So I did.

I raised a flame in my hand. I made it barely hot and mostly hot and very hot and really hot, so that the colors shifted from orange to yellow to blue to white; and as I held that flame, second after second, dazzling Henry and Louise, I made it larger and larger and it began to swirl, until, to be honest, it got a little spooky. Even Henry and Louise had the feeling that it wanted to *leap* onto something and burn it. I don't think it would have been a dud, either, not like my impatient burst in the prison. I decided to end the flame; and it ended. Then, a little less ominously, I made a fireball and lobbed it between my hands, more or less juggling. Then I flicked a few blinding sparks at the creek—and scared the steam from the water.

Henry soon decided that I should fly. He cried, "Jake, be a rocket!" The thought *had* crossed my mind. I said, "Yeah, and where would I go?"

"Up. Away. The clouds. The moon!"

Louise poked me. "Oh, Jake! Carry me to the moon!"

She was joking—I could tell by her smirk—but there was also a touch of, I don't know, *romance* in her voice. It's not every girl whose boyfriend can carry her to the moon. And it appealed to me, too, though not only for romantic reasons. It's not every boy who can be a rocket.

So I said okay.

As a rocket, though, I made a good brick.

I could keep the fire alive and swirling around my feet, but when I threw it down to propel me up, it just became a little bomb and knocked me over. So I sort of coated myself in fire, to keep myself and the fire steady, and as soon as I threw down the fire near my feet, I replaced it, and then I threw the replacement fire, and I kept repeating that, to create propulsion—at least, that was the theory. What I actually did was turn myself into a tumbling spastic sparkler. (I even set some bushes on fire, but we put them out.) So I coated myself again and *threw* the fire, hoping it would carry me along; but it couldn't lift me. It ripped.

Nothing worked.

Yet it only seemed *right* that my fire should help me fly. Maybe I had read too many comic books, but nearly every metageek like me could jet and glide on his flames and it just seemed *wrong* that I couldn't.

But I simply couldn't and that was that.

We still kept ourselves amused. And, you know, it's strange how *used* to it we got. Sure, we were a little clumsy. There was my rocket failure, for one thing, and Louise's twisted ankle. But all in all it seemed very *natural* to us—natural even to Louise, who wasn't as hesitant anymore.

We practiced for quite a while.

Then Louise sat down. She took off her shoe to rub her sore ankle. She realized she wanted to stop doing metathings, not for any *deep* reason but just because she wanted to do something else. "It would be nice," she said, "if we could be normal for a while." And since it was summer, she suggested a picnic.

Henry didn't want to stop, though. He was stubborn about it. Louise explained how nice a picnic could be. At the very least, we needed to eat. After all, it was almost lunch. Then she said, "Don't you want to be normal for just a while?"

Henry stared at her. "Um. No."

"But a picnic, Henry. In the park. It's lovely out."

"The park is boring."

"It doesn't have to be."

Henry frowned. "The park is far away."

Louise insisted. Henry protested.

I watched the two of them go at it. They weren't fighting, or angry, but both were being a little stubborn, and they went back and forth and got so involved that they more or less forgot about me.

Henry does that often enough, I mean forget about me. Sometimes he gets distracted. The only time that Louise usually forgets about me, even though I'm there, is when she's praying. Oh, she might be praying *for* me, and she's certainly not trying to shut me out—she often invites me to pray as well—but talking to God, or Jesus, or Mary, is a *real* kind of distraction. I can't compete.

But in a way it's all right. She's very pretty when she does it. In fact she gets so far away it's almost like she's a stranger and I'm seeing her for the first time. It's amazing how pretty she is. I get a little embarrassed, even, because I feel like I'm gawking at her. I'm afraid she'll catch me gawking. Luckily, though, I sometimes know how her prayers will end, since a lot of her prayers are the usual ones and she says them aloud; and so I know when she'll be done. Like before we eat she always says grace—and when I hear "Through Christ our Lord, Amen," I know to stop my gawking.

This little argument, though, could go on forever, and I wouldn't get any warning when it was ending. Oh, well. So maybe Louise would catch me. As she talked with Henry, I saw her tug her skirt over her knees. Her legs were bare. Her foot was also bare, because she had taken off her shoe and she wasn't wearing any socks. And then I had the weirdest thought, that her foot was really cute. I had never thought *that* about Louise before.

The thought got weirder. Had her foot *always* looked like that? After all, it had been several different sizes lately.

I looked at Louise. I looked at all of her.

Was that her *original* shape?

Her clothes didn't give me any clues. They didn't look baggy or tight or wide or long. They looked just right. But they always did. Her clothes, you see, grew or shrank as she did. She couldn't change them directly but if she grew something in clothing, the clothing grew, too. This was surely convenient. It was practical. In fact it almost makes you wonder if there wasn't a kind of intelligence in her power. Somehow it knew enough to change her clothes, as necessary. Did her power have its *own* little powers?

It's like with Henry. He can mutate atoms, right? Well, isn't that what nuclear *bombs* do? Every time Henry pulls off his alchemy he should be blowing huge radioactive holes in all of us. He's shuffling around the most dangerous energy in all the universe and for all the fuss it causes, he might as well be rearranging beans. Somehow his power knows how to keep away the nuclear explosions—and it's *able* to keep them away.

My power knows not to burn me.

I wonder if our powers are really like little computers, little machines, little *creatures* just attached to us, and we're only giving them commands—and it's the creatures, not us, who have so much to do and the know-how to do it.

Whatever the case (and I still have no idea), I couldn't tell if Louise was different. Except that she didn't seem to be.

She was as pretty as ever.

I finally interrupted them and said, "Let's have a picnic in my yard." Henry grumbled but agreed, since my yard wasn't far away and he wouldn't have to be normal for *too* long; and Louise agreed, too, since the day was just as lovely in my yard as it would be in the park. So we left the woods, walked a block to my house, made our sandwiches, got our pop, and set down on a blanket on the grass.

As we ate, Henry couldn't resist at least *talking* about metathings. We didn't bother stopping him. It was no big deal, really. He soon brought up our metanames again. He even figured that the three of us counted as a *team*—and our team needed a name, too. His best one was probably "Triple Force," although then he decided that we shouldn't exclude Nina, so he changed it to "Quadruple Force," which I said wasn't quite as good. Then Louise came up with a name that Henry and I thought was a little weird, at least for a team of metahumans. It *starts out* with something of a kick, but then it gets all, I don't know, *girly*.

Still, Louise was stuck on "Thundershine."

She said, "Whenever there's a storm I sit by my window, and I wait for the lightning, but that's not what I'm really waiting for. I want to hear the thunder. Especially when it's just far enough away to hear it coming. The thunder is so *big*. It comes into everything and I realize how small I am. I sometimes forget how small I am. I like to be reminded. And our powers are like that. They're so much more than we are—but they're not natural like a storm. It's as if the thunder, instead of being loud, was *bright*. So I think of *shine*. It's poetic. It's noble. I like how it sounds."

We told her we'd think about it.

All in all, though, we didn't talk that much about metathings. We mostly gabbed about nothing special. We really *were* normal for a while, just as Louise had wanted. Even afterwards, as we sat in my yard and did a few little things—tiny patches of alchemy, tiny dancing sparks, and again a fairy Louise—none of it really seemed so terribly meta. It seemed like nothing more than a summer afternoon with friends.

III

The next day, in the evening, I visited Louise at her house.

Mostly, when I visit, we just visit. We talk, maybe we eat. Lots of times we play games. Louise doesn't have any games with fifty real-time 3-D white-knuckle havoc-filled levels of heavily armed 360° blood-drenched video annihilation. *I* do, and I suppose sometimes my knuckles *do* get white, just like the blurbs say; but Louise's family doesn't even have a game station. They have Scrabble.

But Scrabble can be fun, at least with Louise.

These visits are how we date. Louise is very careful about dating—and her mother is especially careful about me. So we don't *really* date. I don't mind. I know Louise isn't trying to cause trouble. She's trying to avoid it. Not that I'm so dangerous, but I *am* a boy. And, really, I don't care. Date, schmate. Dating looks like a pain to me. It's easier just to be together.

Of course we aren't ever together in *her* room. Louise wouldn't allow that. I wouldn't want it. Just the idea of us alone in *her* room makes me uptight. That'd be like *beyond* a date.

So we were in the living room.

We set up on the floor, across from each other, the Scrabble board between us. Her living room has a bay window. Her mother keeps plants on the sills. The blinds were up, and the sunlight—inside the shadow of the window frame—crossed the floor and climbed the wall behind Louise. It was slowly touching the crucifix that hung there.

We talked as we played.

Louise still has her dolls, though she doesn't play with them anymore; and in fact she has some dolls she never played with at all but only kept for show, fancy dolls with white gloves and tiny pearls and feathered hats. As we were playing she told me that she had closed the door to her room the night before, and felt silly for the longest while and hesitated as always; but finally she shrank her-self and put on the elegant dress from one of her most beautiful dolls. Then she grew herself back to normal. The dress grew with her. Of course, no matter how big, it was still a doll's dress. Louise said it fit her strangely and didn't move well as she turned and curtsied; but even so, it was elegant.

She told me, wistfully, "One of those dresses could work out. Maybe with a little sewing. Some have very nice fabric. I wish I could keep one."

"So why don't you?"

"What would I tell my parents?"

"It's not like it'd be stolen. The dresses *are* yours."

"You know what I mean, Jake. My mother doesn't mind if I buy myself clothes. But you know she'd ask me where I got it. That's the first thing you always ask. *Where'd you get it? How much did it cost?* And what would I tell her?"

"Not the truth."

"Yes, the truth. And then what happens?"

"She finds out you're a metahuman."

She frowned. "I don't know if I want her to know."

There were only a few words on the board and I had six vowels and an *R*. I was scrabbling tiles in my head as I said to Louise, "I don't blame you. I don't want *my* parents to know. It's too weird. But what did you tell them about your ankle?"

"Nothing."

"What, did you tell them you fell down the stairs?"

"They don't know it hurts."

"So they don't know anything happened."

She looked past me, checking for her mom. "No, of course not. And you know what, Jake? I feel like I'm *lying.*"

"But you're *not.*" With my *R* I changed *ate* to *rate.* "Do you tell your parents *everything* you do?"

"No."

"And it's not like you did anything *bad,* right?"

She sighed. "No. No, I didn't." She fingered her tiles. She squinted at me the way she does, squeezing thoughts from her head. She tells me that when she was a baby she had the same sort of squint, but in only one eye, and her father called her his Pirate Girl. I can't quite picture Louise as a pirate. "No," she said, "it wasn't bad. It wasn't anything, really, except maybe . . . Well, we didn't *misuse* our powers, and *that's* good." She put two tiles on the board and got a double-word score. "You know what? I bet you could incinerate an entire city. I could probably pound an entire army into the dirt. Have you ever thought of that?" Actually, I had. Sorry to say, it even appealed to me. She went on: "It's so *much.*"

I sat back. "What are you getting at?" Although it was still my turn, I gave up for the moment. Louise was getting way too intense. Besides, I still had six vowels.

"I don't know." She stared at her tiles, not worrying about Scrabble at all. She said, "I've been thinking about this a lot. Where do our powers *come* from? What *are* they, really? We're not doing *tricks,* Jake. These aren't tricks. These are *miracles. Real* miracles." She gave me this look. It might have been joy. But she was afraid, too, when she said, "Only *God* causes miracles."

"Oh, Louise. God didn't give us these powers. Nina did."

"And *who* gave them to Nina?"

She had me there.

"It *must* be God," she said softly, as in a prayer.

We had our powers, like it or not, and even if Louise's questions got me thinking, in an ugly way, that someone *opposite* God was behind all of this, I really couldn't believe that *anyone* was behind it. I told myself that these things just *happen*.

Louise was sure that God had a hand in it. God was allowing it, in any event. So, for Louise, it was still a test. There's nothing bad in growing or shrinking; there's nothing bad in fire, either, so long as you don't misuse it. And that was the key: using and misusing. She was still determined not to misuse her power. As a matter of fact, as far as Louise was concerned, our powers were an opportunity to shine.

I teased her, as if she wanted to go all out and become a Goody-Two-Shoes Hero and get her name in the papers. She shook her head in that tremble of hers and told me I was being dumb. But then she got thoughtful and admitted, "I *do* want my reward to be greater in *Heaven*. I want to see God as clearly as possible after I die. But I should do good anyhow, Jake, because that is God's work and I want to do God's work."

God's work!

And here I thought we were just goofing around.

◆ ◆ ◆

And then we had a fight.

It wasn't much, certainly not compared to the fight I had the next day with Nina; but it *was* a fight, and our first besides.

I asked Louise if she expected me and Henry to join her in Doing Good. It was just a question, but I guess I sounded less than enthusiastic. That isn't what made her mad, though. She said that, yes, she pretty much expected all of us to Do Good. Or at least try. And would that be so awful? I shrugged. Then I asked her if she was thinking of Nina, too. A Do-Gooder Nina wasn't *real* likely.

And that only gave Louise an opening.

I'm sure she had been thinking about it for a while, especially after the thing in the prison. Slowly she asked me, "Why do you hang around with her?"

"Huh?" I scowled. "I don't hang around with *her*. I hang around with Henry. *He* hangs around with her."

"But you do things with her."

"With *them*."

"But you said you don't like her."

"I never said *that*. She just . . . irritates me. There's something not right about her. I always think—"

"What?"

"I dunno. That she's trying too hard to hate her life."

She looked down at her hands. "Do you hate your life?"

That shocked me. I stared at her, wide eyed. "No!"

"Then why do you *do* all those things you tell me about?" She wasn't angry; she was sad. "Nina takes you and Henry out, and you guys, I don't even know what you *haven't* told me, but the things you *have* told me, you do whatever she's doing—" Louise was flustered. "And if *she* hates her life, what's *your* excuse?"

"I don't have an *excuse*. I don't *like* the things she does." That was only partly true. What I didn't like was Nina's *intensity*. She couldn't just be like the rest of us, a stupid kid on a delinquent lark. Oh, no. She was always some sort of merry agent of doom.

"But you do them anyway."

"So I'm not a saint." That wasn't a nice thing to say. Louise takes the Saints quite seriously. It was almost like I was jabbing her. I didn't mean to jab her, but that's how fights usually go. Quickly I said, "Look, Henry's just my friend, I'm used to Nina, I think she's *way* too *something* and that gives me the creeps, it really does, but she's the one who starts all these things and, I don't know, I just go along."

"You don't go along when I pray."

Louise was yanking me *every* which way. "What's *that* got to do—"

"Nina goes out *hurting* and you join her." Now she was sad *and* angry. "I pray and you just wait for me to get it over with."

"That's not—"

"True."

I squirmed. "Well . . ."

"I know you don't believe," she said. "My mother told me this could be hard. She trusts me but you know she isn't happy about this." There was a long silence. She was twisting her hands together, slowly. "I'm sorry. I'm ruining our game." She looked at my tiles. "It's still your turn."

I've heard that when a girl stops a fight, even if it isn't really over, the smart guy lets her stop it. I certainly don't like fighting with Louise and I could tell she didn't like it, either. No, nothing had been resolved. Even so, we quietly finished our game. We talked only a little bit, just enough to get by; but when I left and headed home, I still wanted to see her again.

The next day, Paul died.

Paul lived one street down from Henry and Louise. The houses on his block aren't as nice as ours. He lived in one of these duplexes, half the house for his family, half for another. We really didn't know him. He was only nine years old and we don't hang out with third-graders. But we knew who he was. He and his friends were always making noises in the streets. Not bad noises, just lots of them. Our neighborhood is stuffed with little kids and they tend to run in busy packs.

I don't know much what he was like. He always seemed to be leading, but I didn't really pay attention. Given what happened to him, I guess he was a little reckless. Then again, he was just a kid. Maybe he just made a bad mistake.

That's not how his dad saw it. They say Paul's dad is a drunk. I don't know where he lives. He came back after Paul was buried and attacked Paul's mom with a knife. He was too drunk to hurt her much. He blamed *her* for what happened to Paul. I know this for a fact because I saw the police take him away and I heard what he was yelling.

I don't think Paul's mom blamed herself much. She was out with her boyfriend the next night, all night. That's what I hear.

I went to see Louise that morning. Our fight the day before had not been any sort of falling-out. Oh, I had *no* plans to resolve a *thing,* and as it was, nothing was resolved; but I was glad to see her and she was glad to see me.

Henry came over and at first I was afraid he might sour Louise's mood. After all, you see Henry, you think of Nina. Luckily, though, Louise likes Henry and has nothing against him. The three of us fell easily into our chatter, there on Louise's porch.

A pack of little kids rode past on their bikes. They were racing. There were maybe eight of them. A couple were hugging the curb, which meant they lost time maneuvering around parked cars; the others were tearing straight up the street. We heard them yelping and laughing and egging each other on, but we only gave them a glance. Then they were out of sight, headed towards the intersection two blocks away.

That intersection is an exit from the neighborhood. There's a light, and the cross street is five lanes—two lanes north, two south, and one for left turns. Everything in this part of town is on that street. There are always cars and always trucks, and all of them are going fast.

Paul was winning the race.

We heard a truck or something screech and groan, but as far as we knew or cared, it was only a traffic noise somewhere up the street. A few minutes later, though, one of the kids was coming back down the street on his bike. It was David, one of Paul's friends. He was up off his seat, standing on his pedals, leaning over his handle bars, like he was trying to outrun his own speeding wheels. He was screaming, "Susan, Susan, Susan, Paul's been hit, Paul's been hit, Paul's been hit!"

Susan is Paul's sister. She's nearly twenty. She doesn't come out of the house very much anymore. I've seen her a couple of times since the accident. It looks like she still cries a lot.

Henry stared at Louise and me. "Did he say what I think he said?"

Louise said, "Yes," and ran off the porch.

Susan, in her car, passed us on the way there. It's a good thing the street was clear. Susan was a bullet. When we got to the intersection and joined the crowd, she was already out of her car and being held by two women. She was dangling and wailing.

Henry whispered to a kid in front of us, "Is he dead?"

The kid said, "I don't think so."

Everyone in the nearby houses had come out. All the kids who had been racing were there, even David, who had returned on his bike. There was another, smaller crowd around Paul. We couldn't really see him. We saw his twisted bike and the blood. Paul had hit the back wheels of a trailer truck. The truck was stopped a ways up the cross street. Traffic was snaking out of that lane. The drivers stared.

Louise turned to me and Henry and said, "We have to help him."

I said, "*What?*"

"We have to save him."

"Do we *look* like doctors?"

"We have *powers*, Jake. We have to—"

"*Wait* a sec," said Henry, his voice low. He all but hissed. "We *can't*. Everyone'll see."

"So *what?*" she cried.

"But what about our secret iden—"

"Oh, Henry, *stop* that—"

"Louise," I snapped, "what are *we* supposed to—"

"I don't know!" Her voice cracked. "But we have *powers*—"

"We *can't*," said Henry.

"Yes—we—*can*," she snarled. Louise *snarled*. "Why are we *arguing?* He's probably *dying!*"

Henry grabbed his forehead. "Okay, okay, okay, *okay*. I could turn his blood—I could make his skin—maybe plastic—"

"I'll go *in*, be tiny," said Louise, "and move his bones—"

"Okay, okay, I'll make glue—bone—fix them—"

"And Jake!" She was pleading. "You seal him up."

Henry cried, "Yeah, Jake! *Cauterize* him!"

I pulled back. "*Wait* a minute! We *don't* know what we're doing. We'll only make it worse—"

That's when Nina showed up.

One of the powers that Nina gives herself is this metasight. She can see things from everywhere. It's like having a trillion TV channels piped directly into her brain. It isn't TV, though.

It's real life. Nina knows what's going on just about anywhere. She doesn't need this information for anything other than its gossip value. Stupid thing is, she has no one to gossip with. Still, she does it.

I would rather not know she can do this. I have felt naked ever since I found out.

Nina had started doing it just a day or so before Paul died. At the time he was hit, she had been eating nacho chips in her room, her eyes closed, her brain drowning in the world. She had caught sight of Henry's street and the crowd and the three of us and, otherwise bored, had decided to come see the accident. She sort of knew Paul, the way we did. He wasn't exactly a *total* stranger, not like all those other people she had already seen die that day, here and there.

Nina appeared beside us. I don't think anyone really noticed. Paul was still the center of everyone's attention.

"Nina!" Henry cried. He was happy to see his sister, but not only that. I think he was relieved. With Nina around, we didn't have to be doctors, we didn't have to come up with a plan, we didn't have to risk making a mess of things. She could fix everything with a thought.

Louise realized this, too. She went right up to Nina and said, "Nina, please help us. Paul's dying."

Nina raised her eyebrows. "I'm sure he's already dead. Did you see how he hit that truck? No, I guess you didn't. I did. At least it's in my memory of sights. Want to see? It's not the most beautiful—"

"*Do* something," Louise yelled.

Nina made a face. "What? Raise the dead? *Geez,* Louise, I do believe you have mistaken me for someone else."

Louise glared at Nina, not with hatred but with this terrible, bewildered sort of anger. "You don't even care."

"That's not my job."

Louise was truly upset. With unusual impatience she spat out at Nina, "You're awful." Then she spun and started off towards Paul.

It is not, of course, the smartest thing to insult someone who could probably erase you from the universe. As it was, Nina was so instantly incensed by Louise that she didn't even think to go meta. She all but punched Louise, grabbing at her shoulder. I saw the grab and tried to block Nina's arm, but I wasn't quick enough. Nina spun Louise around. I was so intent on stopping Nina that I couldn't catch Louise, who landed, hard, on her hip. Nina stared at me, I stared at her, and I still don't know what was in her face. But she didn't hit me or continue after Louise.

"Stop it!" Henry cried.

The people near us realized that some sort of fight was going on. They backed away. I'm sure they were trying to figure out why there should be a *fight* at such a moment, what with a nine-year-old boy dying in the street.

As I helped Louise up, Nina said, "You think you're going to use your power? *Do* you, Louise? To *help* somebody?" She turned to Henry. "And is Worm Boy in this, too?" Henry shook his head, but Nina could tell that even Worm Boy was in-

volved. She said, "You're a bad influence, Louise. I'm tak[
your toy back."

I said, "What do you mean—"

"What do you *think* I mean?"

Louise looked down at herself. She was normal. She stayed normal. "My power's gone," she muttered.

"That was childish," I said to Nina.

"Was it, Jake? I'm *so* sorry." She stepped towards me. "But you still have *your* power. Don't worry."

"I don't *care* about that. Leave Louise alone."

"Isn't that what I'm doing?" She took a very deep breath. Her eyes were bright. "And are you *sure* you don't care about your power? You might need it, Jake. Someday. Or right now."

I felt something *thud* around my feet. It was ice. It was rooting into the ground and clawing up my legs. It clamped on my waist and grabbed at my chest and whirled down my arms. It paused at my neck. Nina said, "We've got a crowd, Jake. Time for that column of flame." Then the ice swallowed my head.

Cold wasn't the word for it. It was like there was no such thing as heat and no hope of it. Everything inside me was just *stopping*. My eyes were frozen open and I saw nothing but the glare of the ice that was killing me.

I had to use my fire. Nina wanted me to use it. I was ready *not* to use it, precisely because she wanted me to use it. But I didn't want to die.

Because I wasted time being stubborn, I was left with only

enough time to panic. I must have ignited myself with a thousand suns—but Nina's ice wasn't water, it was a chunk of blinding *emptiness,* and even a thousand suns only managed to blow the cap around my head. The fire screamed upwards, taking me with it.

I was finally a rocket.

I ended the fire when I realized it was pushing me into space; but then, of course, I slowed down and started falling. I wasn't that incredibly high, maybe a mile or so.

It would hurt, though, when I landed.

I was already hurting *everywhere* from the acceleration. I was falling and spinning. I felt like a tossed-up ball of pulp.

And I was still *so* cold. You know my fire doesn't burn me. I can't feel its heat. I tried to heat the air right around me, but I kept falling out of it. I had to rely on a mild summer day to warm me back from oblivion.

Like it made a difference. Cold or warm, I would be a corpse soon.

I hoped that Louise was praying for me.

I stopped falling.

It was like I was treading water, except I was half a mile in the air.

Then I stopped hurting.

I felt perfectly warm.

Nina flew in front of me. She seemed weightless. Her hair was swirling around her. She was giddy.

"Jake! It was *gorgeous*! Every little flame was *taut* and slicing right up into the sky. The thunder *knocked* people down. And when you first blew out of the ice, the fire *blossomed*. The tops of the trees are burning!" She laughed. "But I didn't expect it to *launch* you. That was a little less than dignified!"

I was afraid to speak. I was afraid my rage would show and Nina might decide to let me drop. But I spoke anyway. Calmly. "Did I hurt anyone?"

"Nah. Not much. It *was* overkill, though."

"Sorry. I was *dying*."

She flitted her hand. "Hardly. You think I'd *kill* you?"

Calm, calm. "I'm not sure what you wouldn't do."

She shrugged. "There isn't much I can't."

"Then save Paul."

She winced. "Oh, please. Are we still on that? I won't."

My hands were fists. My fists were tense. "Then let *us*."

"What could *you* do?"

"I don't know!" *Calm. No rage. No rage.* "We probably couldn't do anything. But Louise is right—"

"No. Besides—" She looked down. "The ambulance is already there. Boy, they're going to need more than *one*. Look at all the people whining from the bumps you gave them! Anyhow—" For a moment, barely a twitch, Nina was silent. "They're covering him. I told you he was already dead. Well. Louise caused all this fuss for nothing."

So, okay. I lost my temper. With a bright white fire I blasted Nina so hard the thunder hurt my bones.

◆ ◆ ◆

I suppose part of me expected her to survive. Or should I admit I didn't care? At the time I didn't. I could say I was out of whack, given what had happened up to then; but that's no excuse, is it? I meant to do what I did. My decision was passionate, maybe, but it wasn't confused. Whether she was hurt or killed was not the point. She *deserved* it.

Why, I wasn't exactly sure. But she deserved it.

And when you do something like that, as soon as it's done, you wonder who it was that did it. It certainly wasn't *you.* It couldn't have been. You don't do those kinds of things.

Or do you?

When I was fighting with Louise and I more or less blamed Nina for the things I did, saying that I only went along, I conveniently forgot that I had done things *without* Nina. Alone, I never did anything half as bad as with Nina; the point is, though, that I didn't need Nina to fail at being good.

It certainly wasn't Nina's fault that I blasted her. She may have been obnoxious, indifferent, heartless, infuriating, whatever you want to call her, but it seems there's something inside *me* that's ready to destroy, given an excuse—and the power.

So my fire hissed away. No smoke, no ashes.

No Nina.

And then she hit me back.

With fire.

And because it wasn't mine, it burned.

But she didn't intend to cremate me. It only hurt. I hovered, still held by whatever she had hung me on, and the stinging danced on my skin.

She was in front of me, as before. Not a scratch or a scorch mark. But she was trembling. "You're lucky," she said. "I saw it coming. It still hit me, though. I only had time to wish I would survive." She smiled slightly. "My *wish* survived. I guess it brought me back."

"You were dead?"

"I don't think so. Just . . . vaporized. Disappointed?"

"No." I felt sick. "I wish I hadn't done it."

"Then why *did* you?"

I was in no mood to talk. "I don't know."

She moved towards me. Her hair whipped slowly around our heads. It touched me and worsened the stinging. "Tell me, Jake."

"You let him die."

She glared at me. "Oh? It's *my* fault he's dead?"

"No. It's your fault you stopped us."

"You couldn't have saved him."

"Maybe not. And maybe we shouldn't have tried. But why did you stop us? And why didn't *you* save him? You could have."

"I thought you knew me better than that, Jake."

I stared at her. Her body had stopped trembling. Her face had not. And she was right. I knew her better than that. I was thinking like Louise.

"This fight's over," she said.

I found myself on the ground, at Louise's feet. She was crying. She saw me and grabbed me and hugged me. That certainly didn't help the stinging, but I didn't want her to stop.

Henry crouched down. "Where's Nina?" he asked. I just looked up. He looked up, too—but Nina wasn't there.

IV

More ambulances were called, and fire trucks, and more police. Before long, the TV crews showed up, too. In the confusion, Henry, Louise, and I tried to get lost in the injured crowd. Of course some people had seen it all, the fight, the ice, the fire; and they said they had seen, who was it, oh yeah, Nina and Henry, what's their last name, and Louise Cavanaugh, that's who it was, and her boyfriend, you know him, Jake. The police soon found us with some paramedics. Henry and I avoided the truth. Louise lied, too, reluctantly, and on top of everything else it only made her more unhappy.

What good would the truth have done, anyway? They wouldn't have believed us.

When they learned that Nina was home and her mom was *positive* that she hadn't left the house, they decided that we weren't really involved. The witnesses had to be confused. Besides, how *could* we have been involved? A column of fire had punched the sky! No explosives, no chemicals; but still, a fire. And the ice? Too unreal. How could *we* be responsible? We weren't *magicians*.

We were just kids.

When I wonder why Nina did what she did, I remember something she told me only a few weeks before Paul died.

She was taking me and Henry out for another of her adventures. She had just turned sixteen. She didn't have her power yet.

The day wasn't warm and Henry decided he needed his hat. While he ran back to his house (we were over a block away), Nina and I were alone on the street. It wasn't the first time the two of us were alone together. Sometimes we get separated from Henry, for whatever reason. And it wasn't the first time she told me things I didn't need to know. I think she waits for chances to talk to me. I suppose if I got obnoxious and really started avoiding her, she'd have no friends at all.

I don't know why I listen. I suppose there's no reason *not* to listen. It's the same reason I keep joining in her little bits of mayhem. No reason *not* to, even if it isn't always pretty. Too much work to end it all.

And it's not like I *hate* her.

She said, "Henry tells me you've got a girlfriend."

I shrugged. "Yeah. I guess so."

"Little Louise Cavanaugh. From across the street."

"Yeah."

"Just caught your eye, huh?"

"I guess."

"Kissed her yet?"

I blushed a lot more than I would have expected. "No."

She laughed. "But of *course* not. Where is it she goes to school? Oh, my, yes. Our Lady Queen of Martyrs. Her kind don't kiss before marriage, do they?"

Nina always manages to remind me why I have an attitude about her.

When I didn't answer, she said, "Don't worry. No one's ever kissed me, either. Sweet Sixteen and never been—" Nina stopped. She got this kind of gloomy she often gets. (A couple of years ago I wondered if that's what a teenager was all about: being gloomy. Now I know it isn't; but listening to Nina so much, I had to wonder.) Much less flippantly she said, "But I'm *not* Sweet Sixteen. You know what Sweet Sixteen is? It's waking up two hours before you have to go to school and washing your hair and sleeping a while longer, upright, so your hair can air dry because blow-drying ruins it. It's having chocolate shakes at lunch but nothing else, because having food, too, would be too many calories. It's having a sleepover with your friends and going for pizza, and not bothering to get dressed, but all of you going out in pajamas and long T-shirts and picking up your pizza from some guy behind the counter who thinks you're a daring bunch of girls. It's being a candy striper at the hospital and volunteering for the orthopedic floor because that's where all the cute guys are, the ones who have had accidents with their motorcycles and skateboards.

"That's what I hear, Jake. What I *overhear*. But I'm not any of that. I'm not even close. I don't *want* to be. I don't *care*. I'm not *anything*. I'm just *stuck* here. I'm not Sweet Sixteen. I'm Half Thirty-Two. I'm just waiting to stop being whatever I am."

That's what Nina told me. No one, I suppose, could be as empty as all that, but Nina certainly acts as if she's only stuck here. She wastes herself on so many useless things. Whatever she truly is, she doesn't like it; she *refuses* to like it. She wants it just to stop—and I really don't think she expects anything afterwards.

I told you she was messed up.

I suppose there's a way to explain Nina. I'm sure there's a whole list of things that made her what she is. The day that Paul died, though, none of that mattered. At that point, Nina was Nina—and when I think about it now, I realize she would never have saved a dying boy. She would never use her own power—or, for that matter, let us use the powers *she* gave us. That's not who she is. It just doesn't fit. I can't imagine her being like that. You don't save someone's life when you don't even care for your own.

Nina was only being consistent by letting Paul die.

I tried to explain this to Louise, in so many words, and Louise tried to understand. It made sense to her, mostly, as much as a girl like Nina can make sense to a girl like Louise; but she also thought there was a little more to it. Louise is sure that Nina simply dislikes her. Saving Paul was *Louise's* idea, so Nina opposed it all the more. That seems petty to me, but it might be true. It would be very *human,* really, and I have never said that Nina isn't human.

To Henry, of course, Nina is not a monster. He hasn't abandoned her. Nina is very lucky. She doesn't deserve Henry, but I suppose lots of us don't deserve the love we're given.

There's one thing, though, that kind of separates them now. They haven't argued about it, they haven't talked about it, and

Henry doesn't know what he will do about it; but he thinks that maybe Louise is right, and if we can't do good with our powers then maybe we shouldn't do anything at all. Unlike his sister, Henry keeps thinking of Paul and what we didn't do.

Of course Louise doesn't have her power anymore. She doesn't *want* her power back, and none of us can imagine Nina giving it back. As for me and Henry, we haven't done anything meta lately. For me, at least, it isn't very appealing. Besides, we decided we don't want to add to the rumors and suspicion in the neighborhood. The police may have already dismissed us, but everyone else still wonders.

Nina doesn't worry. She still does her metathings. Luckily, she hasn't been doing them much around here. Henry says she was dancing on the sun the other day. He also says she was off throwing rocks at dinosaurs last week. She's keeping busy doing nothing.

A while after Paul died, Louise took me to the intersection.

It bothered Louise that Paul's death had gotten mixed up with the fire. It all should have been simpler and everyone's sadness should have been pure. There should only have been a boy who died. Instead there was a big fat Strange Phenomenon, and everyone was getting so kooky about it that they were forgetting to mourn.

She felt partly responsible for this. Of course it was really my fault and Nina's, but Louise wouldn't comfort herself with this. She wanted to make amends. So she went to the intersection when the crowds were gone, to imagine how it would have been, without the chaos of anything meta; and there she would pray.

They had cleaned the pavement as much as they could. I was surprised that it wasn't back to normal. They had covered it with leaves. By then the leaves were pressed down by the wheels of cars. This reminded me that the little kids were saying they had found the truck, parked in a lot nearby, with bloodstains still on its wheels. I doubted this, but the third-graders were taking other kids to see.

I was still out of sorts. I had been taken to the emergency room for my burns. As it was, they hadn't been that severe. Severe or not, they were all over my body and they hurt. The doctors were surprised that I could be so utterly covered yet not so very damaged. They kept me for a while. They gave me drugs. They gave me baths and ointments. They told my parents how to watch over me and scheduled later visits. They sent me home. I wore soft clothes. I tried not to bend too much. I got by.

Louise had wanted me to go to the intersection with her. She could have gone on her own, but she wanted me there. I asked her why. She said she just wanted me there, with her.

We sat on the curb.

She brought out her rosary. "I'm going say a prayer for Paul," she said, and waited for me to reply. I said, "All right." She looked at me a moment before closing her eyes. She kissed the rosary and crossed herself with it, then worked her way from the crucifix, along some of the beads, to the medal. Her lips were moving and I knew what she was saying, more or less (because she's told me what she says); but I couldn't hear her. At the medal she stopped. Her lips were closed. I don't know what she was saying to God at that point. Then she crossed herself and kissed the rosary again. She opened her eye closest to me, slowly, like she wanted to catch me at something. Nothing, though, to catch me at.

"Now," she said, "I want to say a prayer for Nina."

"*Nina*? What for?"

"Don't you think she needs it?"

"She needs a *shrink,* maybe."

Louise sighed. "It's not her head that's sick. I don't know if 'sick' is even the word for it, but something's not right. You said so yourself."

"She won't change."

"She *can*. There must be some—some *spark* in her. She loves Henry, doesn't she? That's a start. And if there *isn't* a spark, then God can give her the grace to change. But someone has to ask him to." She looked at me so calmly. "I want us to ask him."

"*Us?*"

She nodded.

"But I don't know—"

"Just cross yourself and *ask* him."

I stared at her.

Louise had said it so sadly, during our fight: *Nina goes out hurting . . .* Was I going to wait for Louise to finish with her rosary, so we could go do something else? Was that the best I could do? Couldn't I even *try*? She wanted me to try. Did that matter to me, what Louise wanted? Yes. And it's not because I liked her as much as I did. It's just that you look in Louise's face and you can tell she knows something you don't.

So I said, "Okay." Her joy, then, made her even prettier. And it wasn't much, I guess, at least in itself; but I said a prayer for Nina.

I hope that God was listening.

DAVID SKINNER is the author of the critically acclaimed novels *The Wrecker* and *You Must Kiss a Whale*. He lives in Redford, Michigan.